About the Author

The author has been writing novels and short stories for about ten years. The ramifications of love and exploitation and everything in between have been a favorite topic, the main characters getting trapped in tainted love, social misfortune, or bad luck, having to fight their way out of this, sometimes helped by a close friend or even a lover.

Five Star Hooker

Tanya Tuschberger

Five Star Hooker

Olympia Publishers
London

www.olympiapublishers.com
OLYMPIA PAPERBACK EDITION

Copyright © Tanya Tuschberger 2024

The right of Tanya Tuschberger to be identified as author of this work has been asserted in accordance with sections 77 and 78 of the Copyright, Designs and Patents Act 1988.

All Rights Reserved

No reproduction, copy or transmission of this publication may be made without written permission.
No paragraph of this publication may be reproduced, copied or transmitted save with the written permission of the publisher, or in accordance with the provisions of the Copyright Act 1956 (as amended).

Any person who commits any unauthorised act in relation to this publication may be liable to criminal prosecution and civil claims for damage.

A CIP catalogue record for this title is available from the British Library.

ISBN: 978-1-80439-875-3

This is a work of fiction.
Names, characters, places and incidents originate from the writer's imagination. Any resemblance to actual persons, living or dead, is purely coincidental.

First Published in 2024

**Olympia Publishers
Tallis House
2 Tallis Street
London
EC4Y 0AB**

Printed in Great Britain

Preface

My name is Yvonne. I'm the one who wrote this book with a little help from Tanya Tuschberger. It's about me and my best friend Connie and some of the things we've experienced. The first paragraph is something I wrote as a kind of introduction. That's about my life now. Otherwise, it is in chronological order, starting in the year 1967. That's important to keep in mind. Many things were different back then. A bit of everything that has been included. Old stuff I've written about it, a few quick notes I once scribbled down, and a few paragraphs written by someone else from back then. Most of it is something I've written now to tell you about my thoughts of the years back then. I have also included some old notes I made many years ago. And some texts were written by people I knew. It's a bag of mixed sweets. It appears as written in 1998. That's when the interview about my art project took place. I have included what I thought was essential for the context. Some are written with in the first person, others are written in the third person. Maybe it's a little messy, but I've done the best I could. I'm not claiming it's fine literature. It's not that important, either. The most important thing, and what I hope for, is that Connie reads it. It was written for her. It's Connie's book.

Why Do Men Never Call Back

It was late at night. It was long past midnight. Yvonne sighed. Then he probably didn't call today, either. Or rather, yesterday. Which had now passed. But maybe tomorrow. Which was now today. There, he had almost a whole day to call if he bothered to do so.

She put down the wine glass. It had been a long day. And now she felt how tired she was. But maybe he would call today. That is, if he bothered.

She didn't know what to think of him. She had her doubts. Maybe he wasn't the right one after all. But you never knew. Men were so troublesome. But still, you needed them. And he had seemed okay at first. Very interested and everything. But it was not sure he called. There were many men who didn't. Whether it was because they had changed their mind or because they just didn't have the guts for it, that's how many men were.

Once, she had used it as a sign of whether they were worth collecting or not; several of her friends also used it. It was considered a pretty sure sign. If he called back and quickly, there were probably some opportunities in him. If he only called back after a few weeks, he probably wasn't worth betting on. It used to be a sign you could rely on.

It was more complicated now these days. And it wasn't just because she had become older and more mature and had more bad experiences behind her than back then. That was because it wasn't that simple.

There were also those who just stayed away after she had made a very clear agreement with them. It was annoying. Then she sat there and waited in vain. Wasted her time. She hated that.

Men were erratic. You never really knew where you had them. She sighed again. Where were they when you needed them? Now, she badly needed one. And it should be soon. She could feel it. She already had a plan for how she would do it this time. But it was one thing to plan it. After all, the real inspiration only came when she had the man with her. After all, it also had to be adapted to him and the opportunities he held. And it could be very different. It was important that you had a sense of it. Otherwise, as a rule, it became a mess.

She believed that she was rather good at reading men and the possibilities that were in them. Their potential. Most importantly, the possibilities in their body. Their physique. How they were built, how fit they were. Slim and athletic. Small and stocky. Tall and thin. Or too fat. How muscle and fat were distributed. High-stemmed or low-stemmed. Crooked in the back or elsewhere. It was amazing how different the male bodies had been that she had encountered over the years. And the man's charisma, not least. It could be quite decisive. Their personality. Their style. That was very important. There were many things to think of when embarking on a new man.

It was exciting to work with, really exciting. A new challenge every time. She had become good at it by now and had gained great recognition for it. One reviewer had stated that she was one of the best. One of the greatest and most conscious artists in this respect. That she worked more purposefully and carefully than most of the others and, at the same time, was innovative so that it was not just a repetition of the same things. There was a significant line of development in her work. The reviewers attached great importance to this.

She was really an artist in this field. But now she had taken a break a little too long; she thought how she longed to be back in business. But it wasn't always that simple to get the men on board. She was getting impatient. Restless. She turned on the machine. Just to hear the sound and imagine that she was already working on a new man. This was her favorite machine, the one she preferred to work with, especially for the big projects. Approaching, she let the needle spin in the air how she loved that sound. Now she had to get hold of a man. Now she couldn't wait any longer. And not just anyone. A good one. One that was suitable for the exact project she had in mind.

She couldn't wait any longer. She could feel it. She had so many ideas that she longed to realize. Her fingers tingled to take him under loving treatment. She turned the machine back on and poured more wine into the glass. If he called at all, he probably didn't do it right here in the middle of the night. And certainly not if he was a nice and decent guy. All that neatness. All the conventions. She did not bother what time of day it was? She wanted him here right now.

After all, she had been watching him for a while. She had had him on her radar for quite some time. She used to select her men carefully. And this guy seemed like he who would fit perfectly with what she had in mind this time. And he had seemed interested. Seriously interested. But why didn't he call? Why couldn't he pull himself together and get started?

Maybe he thought it was too extreme. Maybe he was afraid that it would affect himself and his whole life too much. She had often experienced this. Men were often worse sissies when it came down to it.

Why was it so difficult to find a useful man today? Someone

who didn't care about all sorts of niceness and prejudice and other people's opinions about such things. Someone who had the courage to just throw themselves into it. Someone who wasn't afraid of something a little extreme or different or innovative but who dared to let loose without knowing in advance exactly where it was going. Someone who dared. One that would go all the way. One that didn't turn around halfway.

Yvonne sighed. She had been disappointed so many times by now. Just when she thought she had found the right one. Then, he didn't want to do it anyway. That was not fair, she thought, when she needed him so much. One that she could give the very best she had, her exquisite art.

The Day I Was Discarded

The day Martin discarded me, I was totally mad at everything. He was too rough. He wanted me to leave almost as soon as I came. Because he had a lot of extra work to do for his job at the university, he said. And a lot of nonsense about why we had to take a break and could I have a good life on my own and so on, and so on. Finally, he hurried to free himself from my goodbye hug and almost pushed me out of the room because, it couldn't go quickly enough to get me out of the door (and of his life). I thought, *What is he up to? What the hell is going on here?*

But some minutes later, when I met that totally blonde and blue-eyed Bambi girl (which was Connie, the very first time I saw her) on the way up the stairs, just as I was on my way down and had reached the first floor, and she stops and asks me, "Do you know if a guy called Martin lives here, and what floor is that?"

Then I did not think any more. I just reached my tongue at her and hissed. "It's not here. It's in the next stairwell—down in the garbage room."

And she just stood there looking at me totally uncomprehending and Bambi-innocently. And I still did not think at all because why on earth should I bother, so I just continued like a robot down the stairs while she continued upwards in the direction of Martin´s apartment.

That was when I first met Connie. These were the first few words I said to her. We have often laughed about this later. Once, when we were a bit drunk, we talked about both having it done as a tattoo that showed that we belonged together. It also would have been a little naughty because, in the mood we were in, it had to be down over the cunt, addressed to all sorts of Martin types, and then it should say, *Do you just want a quick fuck? Then you've gone wrong! It's in the next stairwell, down in the garbage bin room!*

It would have been a crazy thing to do. I am glad we didn't.

But the day when Martin has kicked me out, and I've passed by that Bambi blonde, and when I had climbed all the way down the stairs and managed to get out into the street, I still did not think. I just continued along the sidewalk like a mechanical doll. When I got to a side street a little later, I still wasn't thinking. I just mechanically followed the street corner into the street.

By the time I had reached about half a mile down the side street, I still wasn't thinking. I just wasn't in the mood for that cumbersome stuff they call thinking. It was not even because I thought it be of no use. Rather, as a kind of assertiveness, I did not want to waste my time on such a stupid thing like that. I made a point of being completely empty and blank. I was not thinking about anything. I acted. I went drinking. And I mean serious drinking.

At the first random tavern I encountered. It was a completely trashy sort of beer joint. All the other guests were men, except for two women who were a little more than half-old and a little more than half-drunk and would not have been a good advertisement for anything, not even themselves.

If I still had been thinking a little, I would have been depressed by this place. Therefore, it was very convenient that I did not think at all. Easy way to solve that problem.

It was kind of weird, but I watched all the ugly stuff in this place, right down to the detail, much more accurately than usual, but I didn't care. All though I could easily see how disgusting it all was. But it's like it didn't really concern me. I just sort of recorded it quite soberly, like a camera. Nice and easy. I felt almost invulnerable. Nothing could touch me. I didn't think anything could shock me or put me out of my composure.

I had already gulped down the first beer. I needed that. I grabbed hold of the waiter and ordered another one. And then it went on from there. I started pouring down beer as fast as I could.

There was this guy sitting there watching me, but I just couldn't take care of that. He didn't exactly look like a fatherly type who was worried about my health. But frankly, I didn't care. He could stare at me as much as he wanted. No problem.

And yet, not quite. A little while later, he got up and came over and sat down at my table. Just like that, without further ado. I hadn't invited him. He didn't even ask. He just sat down. He started out with some ordinary small talk. But I wasn't in the mood to talk. I think he took that as an indication that I was deeply depressed or something and needed to be cheered up. He introduced himself as Kenneth and asked for my name.

"What is a nice girl like you doing in a place like this?" he asked. Frankly, I didn't want to answer that. Just shrugged my head.

Then he continued, "You look like you need something to comfort yourself with. Has some guy treated you badly? A cute girl like you? That's a bloody shame. Can I buy you a drink or something? he continued. "You know that saying that it's better to sit and cry in the back seat of a Rolls-Royce than in the back seat of a Volkswagen? Maybe I can help you a little with that. Are you interested?"

Then he took out his wallet and started counting hundred-dollar bills. At the time, it was considered a rather large banknote. That was in 1967. today, the money is probably worth ten or twenty times as much. He quietly counted hundred-dollar bills, thirty in all, and bundled them with ten in each bundle and placed them in a neat little stack in the middle of the table between us.

"Is that something that could tempt you," he asked.

I was almost speechless. What was all this about? Did he offer me $3,000? Just like that? What should I do in return? I was a big question mark. But a little curious. And still so angry that I was ready for almost everything wild and crazy.

It appeared that he had guessed my thoughts.

"What you will have to do in return isn't that bad," he said. "Want to hear what it is?" I nodded.

"It's very simple," he said. "Your job is to take care of my guests and pamper them a little. Let's put it this way. Have fun with them, be nice to them, make them feel good so that they are happy and satisfied and much easier to do business with. I think you understand what I mean. And maybe also give myself the same treatment from time to time if I need to de-stress a little after a hard week. What do you say? Are you interested?"

I shrugged, trying to look cool and disinterested. "Maybe—maybe not," I said.

"Fine," he said. "I have a little love nest nearby. A couple of streets away, to be more precise. It's not very far from here. You can dispose of it free of charge if you accept my offer. Of course, you will get paid every time. Doesn't that sound like a very good deal? You're just the type I'm looking for, with just the right charisma. I think you're just as fond of men as they are of you. Am I right? It is so obvious. Maybe some guy just let you down and treated you like rubbish? Then you can take revenge on him every time you lie down and enjoy yourself with one of my guests. And on top of that, make good money from it. What do you say? Should we go and look at the place?"

He interrupted his long stream of speech and looked directly at me. He raised his glass. " Cheers to a good cooperation," he said.

Involuntarily, I also raised my glass. We clinked.

"I think you're just the right person for it," he said, looking at me again with that searching look.

"I don't really know," I said, looking down at the table. Why the hell was I not able to think clearly any more and just reject him and ask him to leave? That's probably what I should have done. But it was as if several different conflicting thoughts were fighting for space in my head.

He looked at me again. "It's only a part-time job," he said. "A couple of times a week, three times maybe. At most, four or five. And it's not an all-night thing, not every time. That doesn't sound like a particularly difficult task for a girl like you, does it? And think of all the benefits of this arrangement. Your benefits. You get paid for it, of course. And I'm not the greasy type if you deliver the goods as you should. I would say that you do not need to have a job on the side. And if you just take proper care of my guests, then you can use the place as your own little love nest. You can bring all your own guys here and make all the money on them you want. I don't get involved in that. I'm not a pimp. I am a businessman. So sometimes there are some customers who need to be looked after and cared for and lubricated a little with some female company. Then, it is often much easier to close a deal. But I need to make sure you're always there when I need you and that you stand up to serve my guests, even if some of them have some slightly more special requests that are a little wilder than the missionary position. I'm sure you can find out. I or my secretary will call and let you know, and then I expect you to always be ready to clear your calendar and cancel any other appointments you may have, perhaps at short notice."

"The 3,000 dollars you get now is a kind of starting fee. But don't go out and use them all right away. It is nice to have a little in reserve if I or my guests should not be satisfied with you and your services. You don't have to worry about your workwear. This has already been taken care of. It's all there. You probably use a regular clothing size, it seems? Fine. Well, I'll need your shoe number. Size twelve, you say? Fine. My secretary will arrange for the necessary footwear to be purchased, which will then be delivered one of the next few days. Should we go there and have a look at the place?"

We did so. It was a rather small apartment situated in a backyard. But it seemed that there was what was supposed to be, of what you needed. And quite a few things more. You just had to get used to the way the place was decorated. It simply looked like a mini version of a brothel from an old movie. That is the only way to describe it. Real voluptuous and vulgar and almost completely exaggerated, like something from a movie or a play. In the closets, there were a lot of rather extreme hooker clothes in different versions. Most of it didn't leave much to the imagination. The furniture and the whole décor were in the same style. In addition, there were a few other, more special things that I didn't really understand until later. It was all quite extreme. But apparently, that's how he liked it and how his guests wanted it. It was not my style. What was it that I was getting myself into?

But I was still so furious that I had been rejected in favor of that Bambi blonde, so I would do this for full measure, just out of pure defiance and anger. Besides, I could use the money. This would solve a number of problems. And I might as well admit that I'm not a saint with that kind of thing.

But what kind of guy was he, that guy? He seemed a little shady. Where did he get all that money from? I thought back and forth. Should I accept it, or shouldn't I?

Then, he tore me out of my deliberations.

"You can just think about it while we're making love," he said. "Or maybe afterward, when we are finished, if you are not into multitasking. It's all up to you. Some women are better at thinking after sex. I see you're up and running right now. I should probably have foreseen that."

Of course, he had to test how good I was in bed. He did.

I let him do it. I even gave it my all, with all my anger toward Martin and her blonde as the driving force. This guy was almost Martin's total opposite. But so much the better. There certainly wasn't that much hypocrisy about things. I was a big fan of that right now.

When we were done, he put on his clothes and asked, "Do we have an agreement?"

"Yes," I said, "we have an agreement." And I reached for the money, which he waved around my nose.

" And you are aware of the conditions?" he asked.

"Yes, Sir!" I said, saluting. Or rather, a botched imitation of it. Suddenly, I had to restrain myself so as not to get laughed at the whole situation. I was still drunk, not to say heavily intoxicated, after everything I'd been drinking in that pub. With what I experienced as a huge effort, I managed to keep my mask on and avoid surrendering to the laughter.

He threw the money by one on the bed where I was still lying.

"I'll find my way out," he said, adding as if it were just something he remembered: "By the way, here are the keys. The one with the red thing on is for the front door. There are a few pieces of paper with the details of our appointment; they are on the kitchen table. Read them carefully, just for your own sake. And here are the keys," the guy said, throwing them at me. But he didn't throw very well, and I grabbed even worse. As a result, they landed on the floor. I didn't care. I stayed put. He was already out the door and gone. Soon after, I fell asleep and had a few rather strange dreams.

The next day, I was heavy in the head. Very heavy in my head. And throughout my body. Real solid hangovers. But I wanted to go to the university lecture. It should all be as normal as possible. Business as usual. I needed that. Then, I had to deal with all this new stuff that had happened a little later. I hurried as much as possible with my morning things and only had time for a very quick look around the apartment before rushing off so as not to be late.

It wasn't until my lunch break, when I had come to sit at a table by myself that I began to wonder about a few of the small details in the apartment. Like for example, a long metal chain that was bolted to the wall. Or the metal brackets on the bed. And what looked like a tattoo machine hanging from a chain from a hook on the end of a bookcase. Or whatever it was. And three or four more things. Was it a normal thing to have that kind of thing in a love nest, as Kenneth had called it?

One of the slightly mischievous guys on the team, whom I would normally never give a second glance, came over and sat down across from me with his lunch tray.

"I guess I can't tempt you with a little drink," he asked, pulling a small mini bottle with some liqueur stuff out of his jacket pocket. He held out the bottle to me so I could read what was on the label. Parfait d'amour, it was called.

"No thanks, I don't usually drink that kind of liqueur," I said in order to get rid of the guy right away. But it was true. I've never liked that sweet, wobbly liqueur stuff. But on top of that, I was so much focused on normality today. I didn't used to be like that.

But I quickly changed my mind and instead said in my sweetest and most flattering voice, "Thank you, I would like to."

"You also look like you need a little strengthening. By the way, my name is Michael," he said and suddenly acquired a facial expression as if he thought he was starring in a movie about the Knight on the white horse.

Or was it just the solid backslide I was still wearing that played tricks on me? It was perhaps a little bigger than I had first thought. At least now, it made itself felt and reminded me that I hadn't finished taking revenge on Martin. The schoolmaster student from Uni, who thought he could teach me how to learn anything when he himself was just a pitiful half-studied braggart and recreational fisherman for cheap blondes of the kind that come in shoals and are so many and so easy that they can be shoveled up by hand and thrown out again after use.

Now, I suddenly knew how to do it. A little extra joyful revenge. Or the feeling of it, at least.

So, when the guy handed me the little bottle of the purple liqueur, I accepted it and said cheers. I put the bottle to my lips and emptied the contents into my mouth, just as he had done with the first half of the sweet stuff.

It probably wasn't just because there were no liqueur glasses on the table. The guy probably thought it was more 'intimate' that way. I didn't even bother asking.

Fortunately, it was a very small bottle.

I lifted the empty bottle and took a closer look at it. 'Parfait d'amour' it said. Perfect Love or something like that. Well, that was perfect. Absolutely perfect, I thought in my afterburn. The perfect revenge on Martin.

To sit here and drink sickeningly sweet and purple Parfait d'amour liqueur with the most mischievous guy in the whole part of the University that I knew of and pretend that I had been so awed by the intimate liqueur drinking that I was almost ready to throw myself into the gauntlet for him

"I haven't tasted something like that before. It's real good," I said in my best sugar voice. Totally hypocritical. And immediately added, "You don't have another one, do you?" Of course, in the hope that he probably hadn't, so we could just grab a beer and drink it normally from separate glasses.

But he cheated on me. I should have foreseen that.

"Sure," he said, smiling much more than was appropriate and then pulling another one of the small bottles out of the pocket of his tweed jacket with a slightly too brisk hand movement, which caused one more of the small bottles to go out of his pocket and fall to the floor right in front of one of my feet. But, of course, the bottle did not even break.

Now there were two bottles, one for each, so we didn't have to drink from the same bottle.

But no. Of course, we should. He immediately stuffed the floor kisser back into his pocket with a suspicious clinking sound. It soon turned out that he had both pockets in his tweed jacket filled with the little bottles of fluffy purple perfect love. Just in case he had to meet a delicious roast. Could he ever—and I mean ever—have scored on it? These are the kinds of questions that can pique my curiosity when I'm in that mood.

But apparently, it was a regular part of his mating ritual with that intimate liqueur splash where you had to drink from the same little bottle as a symbol of some nasty boy-scouting romance.

He handed me the bottle.

"Now, it's your turn to drink first. But only half of it," he said.

Oh my God, this is getting better and better, I thought, smiling big and hypocritical.

For a moment, I thought about taking him to my new pink room and giving him an experience that he could use to masturbate to the memory of for a long time to come. But then I calmed down. Because I basically didn't want to do that anyway.

That Parfait d'amour stuff just harmonized miserably with my hangover, and the more of them I just thought about drinking, the worse it got. There was only one thing to do.

I said nicely, "Thank you for sharing it with me," and a few small friendly phrases so as not to upset the guy, and then I limped home to sleep it off. I suddenly felt a great and urgent need for this.

But hey… my brain thought, as I waited at a red light at a busy intersection… a busy intersection like myself… had I really already considered that pink brothel bubble as 'my home'? No, it was probably just because it was so nice and easy nearby, so it was by far the easiest place to drag my big, weighty hangover right now. That had to be why. So just pure convenience. It wasn't because I had already started to see myself as someone who belonged in such a place. It was just sheer laziness. Nothing else. That thought calmed me down a bit.

Afterward, I thought about it for a moment. Was it so that these were the three types of men that existed? Martin, Kenneth, and Michael. Wasn't there any other kind of men around?

Connie and Me

And that was the prelude to me getting to know Connie. That's one of the most important things that's happened to me. Although it happened in a rather backward kind of way. I'd better tell you a little more about it.

I was on my first round of social rehabilitation. I went to a high school. Probably not the world's best high school. But I got my high school diploma. And then, I became a student at the local university. I started studying psychology. It was quite a fashionable profession. I had noticed a very beautiful blonde girl in my class. But otherwise, it was mostly Martin that I was preoccupied with. It was one of the young hourly teachers, or teaching assistants, who taught many of the subjects. He immediately became my great hero.

And soon after, we also became lovers. It was really hot. I loved him. I slept with him quite often. I still had my dorm room, but I spent a lot of time with him.

But then, after three or four months, that changed; he was suddenly so busy, so it didn't fit as well this weekend. All sorts of excuses. Without him making a clear statement anyway. Until he did, and then I found out why. Another girl had come into the picture. A rival. And it was Connie, the blonde one. Now, suddenly, she was the one in the heat. His new favorite love doll. And she seemed like she was completely infatuated with him, too.

She was really a cute little lamb from a small town. Sweet and innocent. Much more than me. And four years younger.

Apparently, that was what he had fallen for. I hated her!

But there was nothing to be done. Connie loved him as much as I did.

It was very hot between them, too, and they made no secret of it. But four months passed, and then Martin suddenly found a new one, that is, a third one, and then Connie went out in the cold just as suddenly as me. And then suddenly, we had something to get together about, Connie and me. And we did. We were both mad at him. We quickly became best friends.

Connie lived in a rented room with an old lady, and the lady didn't want her to come home later than eight o'clock in the evening. But now I had that pink brothel apartment where we could be together the lectures at the university until she had to go home to an old and worried lady who was probably someone her parents knew.

The Night with the Sailors

And then there was that fatal night. Yes, it was a fatal night. It just went completely off the rails. I wish we had never gone there. But we were young and wanted to have fun. But none of us had been in this part of the town before. And that tavern was really awful. It was early July. We had just had a summer vacation from our studies. We were only freshmen. And now we were going out into town to have a good time. After some hesitation, we went into one of the taverns, a basement tavern, and here we had a lot of male glances thrown at us. We rushed to find a free table in a corner where we could be undisturbed and ordered a beer each. We were somewhat shy about it all. We had heard so much about it being a tough environment, but it now seemed quite calm and peaceful, although some of the men at the other tables were a bit loud. But what? It was Saturday night.

About half an hour, something started to happen. Suddenly, a whole bunch of sailors entered the tavern. I think it was a whole ship's crew from a coaster or something like that. They were already in the vow mood. There were a few of them that were really nice and charming. They talked and laughed and rattled off jokes, and some of them were both funny and quite naughty. The sailors were so loud that we could hardly avoid hearing what they were talking about.

A little while later, one of them came over to Connie and me and asked if they could offer her a drink over at their table. Connie immediately hurried to say yes. She had her most radiant smile out. And I thought, well, what the heck.

We sat down at their table. They had already made room for us where we would be sitting. Connie got to sit on one side of the table between someone named George and the most beautiful of them all. His name was probably Jimmy. And then they had arranged it so that I would sit on the other side of the table and down the other end so I wouldn't sit across from Connie. I would rather have done it otherwise. They were ten men in all. So now we were five men and one girl on each side of the table. They were very generous with both beer and booze.

A few of them were actually quite funny and charming to be with. They were all in high spirits. We actually had a lot of fun, and both Connie and I probably flirted with a few of them as well. Time passed quickly, and we were quite high up, both Connie and I.

But after the first few hours, they began to grow coarse. Real gross, in a disgusting way. It was also getting late. I had become rather irrigated.

But it was like the mood had turned, and the mood had become harsher and rougher. It seemed like they expected something from us in return for all the beer and booze they had been pouring on us all evening. Gradually, they groped us uninhibitedly on both breasts and buttocks and thighs and all. Sometimes, several at once. Also, a few of them that I hadn't been so fond of from the start. There were three or four of them that seemed more hard-boiled than the others. They had all gotten drunk by this time.

I didn't like the way it turned out. Neither the mood nor the harsh tone. It wasn't exactly what I had expected. This didn't look good. It was time to go home. I told Connie what I thought.

"Connie, let's say thank you for tonight and go home now," I said. But when she finally perceived it through all the noise, she didn't want to go home. She was still enjoying herself and hadn't even realized that the mood had changed. She was in high spirits and completely up and running. She laughed and giggled. I think she had had more to drink than me. She was very drunk. That was only one more reason to go home. But I couldn't convince her. She had also almost fallen in love with the biggest and most handsome of them; Jack was his name, whom she sat and cuddled real lovingly.

But I wanted to go home, and it had to be now. And I wanted Connie with me. She just didn't want to. I walked around the table to where she was sitting and wanted to drag her along. But I couldn't convince her with arguments. She didn't understand the situation. She was too young and inexperienced. Too gullible. And too drunk. After all, she was not used to drinking. I made another attempt to get her on board. But she still wouldn't.

Now, those sailors started to get annoyed about it and they got angry with me. I wasn't going ruin their party, they shouted. When I still didn't do my bit to go without Connie, one of them, a young muscle-bulging guy, grabbed me and lifted me up, and even though I was flailing my arms and legs, he simply carried me out of the tavern and threw me on the sidewalk outside.

Connie was still in there. Perhaps I should have made another attempt to get her on board. But it probably wouldn't have been any use anyway. At the time, I didn't know how things would turn out later. But I feared the worst. I probably should have stayed there—or gone back—to support her. I have often thought about this later.

What Ulla Wrote

I've found a few pieces of paper here. It is someone called Ulla who wrote it. She was also in the community back then. She wanted to be a writer. She wrote a diary about some of what she experienced. This must be something she wrote after hearing Connie talk about that famous night when we went drinking. Afterward, when a while had passed. Later, Connie would often catch the attention of everyone when she told a rather exaggerated story about it at some party, when she was drunk. She would try to turn a tragedy into something wild and breathtaking, but still harsh and maybe shocking for some listeners. But it has probably been much worse for her than that. But she probably wanted it to sound a little more harmless than it was when she acted like that. And you have to imagine that it's Connie, something more than half-drunk, sitting in a pub and telling the others who are listening. Maybe it was just her way of trying to cope with it. Some years later, she would even turn this kind of storytelling into some kind of moneymaker when she was broke. I also have some other sheets of paper with some of the things Ulla wrote at the time. I have no idea what became of her later on. I heard Connie talk about it in much the same way at the time. But here's what Ulla wrote. You should imagine that it is Connie who is saying or thinking all this. I think that's what Ulla meant when she wrote it.

Connie, the Next Day

It was the next day. I was lying on my bed. I had been sleeping. Just woke up. It was well into the day. I felt a little weird. I had a headache. I couldn't remember how I got home. I had a pounding headache. I tried to get up. I wanted to get up and sit on the edge of the bed. I felt dizzy. Oh my god, what was that thing on the floor. I must have thrown up when I got home last night. Someone must have helped me to get home. But I don't remember. I have a hangover, of course. That is why. I also got a little plenty to drink. Maybe I'm still a little half-drunk. In fact, I think so. I remember being drunk last night. We went and dangled so much fun while singing. We went crazy and people glanced at us, but we didn't care about that. At some time we moved on from one pub to the next. We took them in a row. Every tavern and beer joint.

Yvonne had gone home, so it was only the sailors and me. We had a blast. There was one of the places where the tap was broken, so the beer kept splashing out of it and onto the floor if you didn't hold a glass underneath all the time. One of the sailors wanted me to hold my mouth under the tap and drink directly from the beer that was pouring out, but I just got all soaking wet with beer all over, so my blouse clung to my body. And when the sailors saw it, they were absolutely thrilled and said that it should be celebrated because now I had been baptized as a newbie harbor girl.

But then there comes a period of time when I can't remember

much, only small glimpses. My problem is that when I get something to drink, I become so affectionate toward all men who are around. And especially that time. I wasn't used to drinking, so it didn't take much to get drunk. And those sailors took advantage of that. And I was still too naïve at the time. I just thought they were cute and funny and nice. There were two of them in particular who were really good at telling jokes and naughty stories. In the end, I could hardly stop laughing. There were also some of them who raved about me, but I just thought that was funny.

I cheered them on in turn. I was really excited, so they could easily catch me off guard. I was also flattered that they all loved me. I wasn't used to that. I thought of myself as the big star of the Evening or something like that. They could easily get their way with me. I was naïve. And drunk. It must be what the hippies of these days call free love. One of the sailors also said so. But it annoys me a little that I can't remember much about those hours and what exactly went on as long as I haven't done anything really embarrassing. It's so weird when you can't remember something like that, and then you meet someone who remembers it and tells you about all the super embarrassing things you've done in a firefight. Or that they claim you have done. They can claim anything, and they won't accept your denial. But I probably won't meet any of those sailors again.

But what is it? I've also soiled my blouse. Oh, how disgusting that is. I'd better take it off right away. I'm a little dizzy still. But I get up, I peel off my blouse and throw it into a corner. But what the heck is that? It looks strange. What happened? It looks like tattoos, yes, here on both of my breasts, actually. A few roses and some small flowers, and then there's something in writing. A few names, maybe? Well, it must be some of the guys from tonight. The sailors. Yes, of course. That must be why. But when did I get all this done? And why. I don't quite remember.

I remember something about Johnny wanting to go and get a tattoo. I also remember something about us walking out of the pub and onto the street. Just like that in a flash. But then I don't really remember anything anymore. But I was getting tattooed at the same time.

I must have been like that. Is it some name, or what is it? I don't remember anything about that. What the hell have they been up to? It's hard to read what it says. It's upside down when I look down. I get all dizzy.

I go to the bathroom and look in the mirror. I think this is very strange because I don't remember anything about it at all. I stand right in front of the mirror in the bathroom to get a little overview of myself and what has happened. Hey, there's also something on the upper arms and here on the stomach. Oh my god, they've really been harsh with me. It's strange that I don't remember anything.

Whew, I'm dizzy. What the hell have they done to me? I'm so dizzy that I must lean on the wall, but now I will try to see what it says, that writing on my skin.

It's still hard to see what it says. Now it's mirrored. What does it say here? Connie and Johnny. Yes, Connie, it's me, and Johnny, yes, of course, it was him with those funny stories he told. I giggle a little when I remember one of them. Well, what does it say? So here, Brian, Kim, and Bjarne. Bjarne, was it the redhead? And Bjorn, it was the one with the beard. And there are still more—Bruno, it says. Which of them was that? All those names don't mean anything to me. But it must be some of those other sailors. But when did I get it made? Have I really been that drunk? There are also a few flowers and hearts and a butterfly and everything.

Whew, I'm dizzy. I guess I'm still a little drunk. Or a hangover, of course. Oh, that headache. I must have something to strengthen myself on. There's a beer here. Yvonne says I become so loving to the men when I get something to drink. It's fun, I always think. I just let them do everything they want to me. Heck, yes. I'll have to stop drinking so much. Whew, maybe I should just lie down and try to sleep it off.

Connie's Got a New Worshipper

Here's some sort of diary entry I found. It's from—what does it say—it's a little rubbed—but it must be from her first days as a hooker. I didn't get into that until a little later. After all, I had my pink apartment and continued to study psychology for another year or so. But gradually, I spent more and more time with Connie and the other girls and became part of the environment myself. The university study never came to fruition. Not for me and not for Connie. But here's the old memo from that time:

Connie has a worshipper! I think that's how you can call it. It's a younger, very well-dressed man who comes and buys her every afternoon. Almost all weekdays, at least. A real nice guy. He looks like someone in a managerial position.

He apparently works in an office on one of those streets behind the theatre.

It's in the late afternoon that he comes along. Same time every day. It must be when he's on his way home from the office. He walks across the bridge over the canal. He comes right by where Connie is usually standing at that time of day.

You'd think there were enough ladies he could get his hands on without having to pay for it. Someone like him. And he probably also has a wife at home. Or maybe he just got divorced? Maybe that's why. But it almost seems like he's fallen in love with her. That is what has happened. I think there can be little doubt about that.

I think she's a little attracted to him, too. I must ask her about it. He is both handsome and charming and probably quite wealthy. I also see him when he comes walking along every afternoon. But it's always her that he wants to be with. Only her. If there is someday when she's not standing there when he comes, he just moves on. He hardly gives the rest of us a glance. I'm usually standing there myself and watching it.

But at least he's different from the usual pub guests or the other drunks. Of course, it may just be the kind of fancy idea he's got, which might last a few weeks or a month, and then he's had enough of it when it. But it's going to be kind of exciting to see how it will develop.

He Belongs to Connie

Some more words from the old diary. This time, it is from about six months later.

That Jansen guy (that's what his name is, that nice office man) has now been with Connie for several months. Almost every day. That is a little unusual. One of her regular daily customers.

But maybe he still needs a little change?

What happened was that Connie had a severe cold and a case of the pelvic inflammatory disease this winter. She's had to hold the bed for a while. She's been off the street for weeks. That's what can happen to most of us when you're standing on the street in too little clothing to make it look naughty enough to attract some customers. But she has been quite hard hit by it. She started walking on the street again before she had recovered properly, and then she got a new round that was worse than the first.

During the weeks that she was off the street, Jansen started coming to see me instead! Now Connie has recovered and is back on the streets, but he continues with me anyway! Maybe he needs a little variety. Connie is the sweet girl, and some men get tired of that in the long run. After a while, they want something a little more challenging.

I might also be tempted to try to play up to him a bit. I'm the one he gets really hooked on and attracted to, so he gives me expensive gifts and gold jewelry and furs and everything like he's often given to Connie. I think I could chop him off her if I wanted to. I think he's ripe for it. I've toyed with the idea a bit. She's had him for so long now. Then, it must be my turn.

But I don't think I will do it anyway. Not when it's Connie. If it had been any of the other girls, I wouldn't have hesitated for a second. But it's something else with Connie. I think she's seriously in love with him. Real in love, although she won't admit it if you ask her.

I think of her poem. I think she really wanted Jansen as her only customer who comes every day and gets rid of all the drunken men from the pubs. I think she hopes for a future with him. I don't want to ruin that dream for her.

So now I'm starting to be a little more dismissive in my attitude toward him. I don't play up to him. I'm completely cold and businesslike, like a quickie with a hooker who just needs to get it over with. A couple of times, I even said that I hadn't got time for him because I was waiting for another customer with whom I had an appointment. So now I think he has probably got the message and has pulled the horns to him.

Yes! For the past three days, he's been with Connie instead of me. Now, he's walking right past me, just like he did in the beginning. That is a good thing. He belongs to Connie, and I don't want to interfere with that.

A Hooker's Song to Her Customer

That's the title of a poem that Connie wrote back then, and which I think is really about Jansen, even though he was a completely different type than the man in the poem. She had lots of other customers, of course, so the poem is not true at all. But perhaps she thought that Jansen was the only one of them who interested her, while all the others were almost a nuisance and a necessary sort of evil.

But here is the poem she wrote at the time:

It's October and the sky is dark. The sky is full of stars, but the moon is hidden.
While the night watchman walks past, the city streets are deserted.
But we meet in a backyard not far from the factory. You are so impatient, In the desolate backyard.
While I lovingly, oh so lovingly, unzip your dirty trousers and take it in my mouth.
I caress your strong, muscular thighs while you fondle my breasts.
With your strong and demanding hands stained with oil and scars.
Marked by decades of toil in the dark of night, your hands slide down my body, Quivering with expectation.
I'm ready for you.

None of us can wait any longer now.

In a little while, the factory whistle will call you back to a world of iron and steel, and your short break is over.

With impatient hands, you pull my skirt down. It's short and tight to make it easy for you, like the break you have from your job.

In the scorching, seething heat where steel is turned into rods.

And a man can be crushed into a mouse If he is not careful.

But now your hands are on my lap, my panties being pulled down.

By strong and demanding hands, the black panties with lots of lace.

The ones you gave me last year for Christmas and told me always to wear.

You whispered my name so tenderly, one of the names you have given me. You called me your own private hooker, and you got what you wanted.

Now as then and right now and always, your proud and hardened steel iron bar.

Quivering with desire once again, once again.

In the darkness of desolation, my blouse gets stained.

By you and your oil and grease, but it does not matter.

You are soiled from your work, just like me.

You put your stamp, your pattern, your imprint on me and my soul.

A pattern as black and dirty as the night, and our sinful, half-naked lovemaking will end much too soon.

Because you must get back to your job at the factory. But it's our pattern now. You put your imprint on me.

Everyone can see you've been there. Now I belong to you.

Once again, once again.
While the days go by and the nights too and, it will be winter and springtime.
And the days get longer, and the forest turns green, And the night will be warm and soft as velvet.
I will wait for you, night after night, for you are all I have got.
My only regular customer.
You will be here again every single night because you work on the night shift. You're on an all-nighter, just as me
I was made for you, and you alone.
You say it so tenderly when you take me again in the deserted place of a backyard.
Once again, once again.
While the moon goes behind a cloud, it's still a long time until morning.
And the shrill sound of the factory whistle will soon be calling you away from me.
And back to your servile job. You are a hard-working man.
Whether in the heat of the iron foundry or in the darkest heart of our backyard.

A Christmas Drama

Sorry to say, but there was that affair with the oh-so-nice office manager who maybe wasn't quite so nice after all when it came down to it. What was his name? Yes, Jansen, his name was. Robert Jansen. That's his name. He was employed by some fine old posh company. The company's office building was somewhere in the neighborhood.

And when he had to go home from work, he had developed the habit of walking by foot to the nearest subway station, which was a couple of miles away. When his workday was finished, he walked across the bridge over the canal to the street with all the sleazy taverns and beer joints. This was also where a lot of hookers were, some of them standing outside the taverns looking for customers. Back then, in 1967, it was a sort of red-light district. That's where Connie and I were. I have watched him come walking by many times. He walked with brisk, resilient steps as if he was enjoying that walk after sitting down in the office all day.

He could hardly avoid walking right past Connie when she was standing on a street corner or outside a tavern. That was the way he first met her. And then he fell in love with her. He was completely obsessed with her and gave her all sorts of expensive gifts. Jewelry and furs and everything.

In a short time, it almost became a regular routine for him every day. In the afternoon, on the way home from work, he just had a quick cuddle with her. Every day for a few years. He must have really been hooked on her. But in the end, it cost him both marriage and career. And all his nice bourgeois life. He was otherwise skilled enough and had worked his way up from a very modest start, and he had been given a trusted position in an illustrious old company. And then he put it all at risk and lost everything. He started to drink heavily. For a time, he lived in a homeless shelter. I don't know what has become of him later.

But for several months, it was all high and dry. I think they both enjoyed it very much. But then he got this idea of inviting her on a great dream vacation in Hawaii or somewhere like that. No, the Caribbean it was. I don't remember exactly where in the Caribbean it was. But that wasn't until he'd known her for a few years. And when they got home from there, it all cracked. After all, he had taken off the till of that fine old company to afford all those daily love hours with her. He paid for it every time. And he kept doing that. And then there were all those expensive gifts he gave her all the time. She must have almost spun gold on him for as long as it lasted. But it was not the money she was after.

It wasn't much that I saw of her during that period, though. I had been put into some re-socialization, where I had to go to a teacher training college and try to study to become an educator. But that's a whole other story that doesn't really belong here.

It was when Connie and Jansen returned from their dream vacation on some tropical paradise island in the Caribbean that it all fell apart. It was something about the fact that there had been unannounced audits and cash checks while they had been away on that holiday, and then his scam had been exposed. He probably had expected to put the money back before the time when there used to be an audit. But apparently, it came earlier than usual.

And then all that stuff about Connie came to light when they found out that he had gone on vacation with her for some of the money.

He had kept it hidden from his wife, I think, but now she wanted a divorce right away. Of course, he was also fired from that good position he held in the company. But strangely enough, his fraud was not reported to the police. I don't know why.

When his wife threw him out, he moved in with Connie in her small apartment here. I guess he imagined it was going to be romantic, something like Paris and Montmartre and all that kind of stuff. But that was an illusion. It didn't last very long. Then, everyday life came along. She can't bear to make love to him at night because some of the men have been rough, drunk, or both and have been harsh to her so that she's disgusted with men and sex and just needs to get everything of that sort of thing over with.

This took place way back around 1970. Back then, it didn't happen as much in cars as it does today. At least not there. It's not the kind of street you drive through. Not everyone had a car back then, either. It was mostly in the pubs that it started. There, we met the men. Or out on the street, simply. But otherwise, in the pubs, where the men were first drinking, and then they fancied one of us girls.

Back then, this was one of the tough pub districts. Now it has become much more touristy. Back then, it was more about sailors and drunken men and naughty ladies and a lot of young and middle-aged and half-old men who went serious drinking. And then there were the tattoo artists, for whom this place was famous as one of the few places where you could be tattooed. Back then, there weren't tattoo shops everywhere.

I happened to get out of the environment rather quickly myself. For a time, at least. But that's a whole other story.

Besides, it was not my own decision.

But this is about all that with Connie and Jansen, all the sad and troublesome things that took place just before Christmas. It was while Jansen was still staying with Connie. It did not work out in the long run. And this is how it came to an end.

It was creaking quite a lot between them already. It wasn't at all easy for any of them to live together like that. It quickly became far too little of a romance. Especially for Jansen, I think. After all, he was used to a completely different way of life.

Connie usually started to work in the early afternoon. And then she often continued until about midnight. It was a long day and a hard life. No doubt about it. But I think it was in her blood. She had a restlessness in her. I didn't work full-time myself. But Connie worked hard.

Jansen didn't want to be where she lived when she took her customers home. Usually, he was in one of the pubs most of the day, right up until midnight. He was not quite sober when he came home to her around midnight. To say the least.

They had made an agreement that she should have her last customer before midnight, and then Jansen used to come home around half an hour later. He didn't want to run into any of her customers.

I don't know why he always stayed in that pub all day. He could have gone somewhere else. He could have gone around town like he was a tourist. Or have gotten himself a job. Of course, no one wanted to hire him in a senior position after the fraud he had made. But surely less could have done it. He was not used to physically hard work. He was also quite flimsily built. But there were many other jobs. He could have become a bus driver, for example. I think he was a taxi driver for a while. But I don't think it lasted that long. Maybe it was because he had started drinking even more heavily. Maybe that's why. I don't know.

I think he tried his hand at a few other jobs as well. But it didn't last for long. Maybe he had almost given up at the time, so he just let it go. It may well be that it was something like that.

But it was that special Christmas drama I wanted to talk about. Or the prelude to it, as it was. I think it was like a few days before Christmas, as far as I remember. Or a week or so before. I think it was a Tuesday. Jansen had started at his usual tavern and had been sitting there drinking all day. And Connie had had a pretty good day at work. Only nice and easy customers. Not anyone who was wildly drunk. It was absolutely one of the better days.

And then, late in the evening, toward midnight, she got a customer out of the ordinary. In a good way, that is. He was from San Francisco. I don't know if he was just here as a tourist or more to do business. It was probably mostly the latter. At least he didn't have his wife with him. He traveled alone. He was a film producer. That's what he introduced himself as. His name was George. I was there myself when he came down to the tavern. It was Cap Horn. One of the pubs was called that. That's when he met Connie. I was chatting with her when he came into the pub and just had a beer and sniffed the local atmosphere. I think he was quite fond of places like this.

And then he saw Connie and went over to the table where I was sitting with Connie. And it was clearly she who had caught her eye. No doubt about it. And then he asked if he could sit there. Although there were many available tables where he could have sat down. And then he started asking a lot of questions about this place in town and about us. He had probably immediately seen what kind of girls we were, Connie and I. And I didn't have any problems with that either. Not when we were at work. There weren't any men to be served right now anyway, so that was okay.

It was mostly Connie that he asked about a lot of things. I didn't hear much of what they were talking about because I wasn't there all the time. I also had my own things that needed to be taken care of. Suddenly, a customer showed up. One of the regulars. He knew that I often sat on Cap Horn when I didn't have a customer and didn't want to stand on the sidewalk. One of my good regular customers who always only wanted me, even though Connie and some of the others were unemployed. So, of course, I went with him. And when I had made him happy and satisfied, then another guy, a new one I hadn't seen before, came along and stopped me out on the sidewalk as I was on my way back to Cap Horn and asked if I was available. And then I went with him. He was quite demanding, so it took a little time. On the other hand, he was not greasy with the money.

It was a while before I got back to Cap Horn, where Connie and that filmmaker were still in deep and heartfelt conversation. It was just such an expression that comes to mind. I mostly sat and listened. I also had to wind down a bit on top of the two men I'd just had. Or who had had me and had satisfied themselves in me. Especially the second one. He was the kind of guy you keep thinking about afterward. That will not do. Then, it becomes too strenuous. They need to be wiped off the board immediately so that you are completely blank and ready for the next one.

Maybe that's what had happened to Connie, with Jansen, I think. She couldn't wipe him off the board. She could feel how much in love he was. And in many ways, he was a nice guy who treated her properly. It's not a good thing when a customer falls in love with a hooker. Not only for the man, as the saying goes.

But for the hooker too. No one ever thinks about that. They just talk about it being a bad thing for the man. But sometimes, it's even more of a bad thing for the hooker. It becomes much harder for her to have to be with all the other drunk, dirty, or just totally indifferent men afterward. Not to mention, if she's really got some feelings in a pinch. If she has fallen in love with him. It's a brutal profession if you're not made of hardwood. Then you should not be a hooker.

Well, I gradually became a little more present and heard some of what they were talking about. You could feel that there was some good chemistry between them. She was impressed by him. I would have been, too. And he seemed genuinely interested. I even began thinking that maybe he was a rival for

Jansen, who was still living with her at this time. And Jansen was almost a shadow of what he had once been. But it wasn't because they were flirting. It sounded more like they were talking business or something like that. And now, I don't mean like a man and a hooker. More seriously than that.

Big business. But I hadn't followed it from the beginning, so I was a little curious to find out what it was about.

He was a filmmaker, as I've already mentioned. As it were, I knew some of the movies he had made. Something in the style of Russ Meyer, who is probably better known. Perhaps he is a little-known version of him. That's how I perceived it. He was here to find the new star for a series of films he wanted to make in the Russ Meyer style. And he had spotted Connie as someone who might become a rising star and female protagonist in those movies.

Now, I didn't hear the details of everything he explained to her about it because I had another man who wanted me. One who entered the tavern. Then I had to take care of him. And then, when

I had fixed him and when I was on the way back, one more customer arrived – and one more. Business was going strong. And I had been at it since a little before lunch, and now it was already late in the afternoon. But I took these customers too. I needed the money. That's why it took quite a while before I came back to Cap Horn again. But they had left when I got back there, so I didn't see Connie again until about midnight.

It turned out that Connie had been with that filmmaker all along. He had invited her out to eat dinner in a very expensive place. And then they had been around the city a bit afterward. He had been very generous and had spent a lot of money on her.

But then, just before midnight, or maybe half past twelve or something, they'd gone back to Connie's place. I don't really know why. If he wanted to be with her, they could have just gone to his hotel room. I don't know why they went back to her place. But maybe that was part of his kind of romance. Or something he would use as an inspiration for his films, maybe. A hooker's picturesque apartment, where she lies with the guys or something like blah-blah-blah. It may be that's why.

But once again, I was distracted. Another guy wanted me. It was just a quick and easy thing. But this guy he wanted his name tattooed on me afterward. And he would pay me extra money for it. I had stopped doing it at the time. In the past, I had done it a few times because it was easy money to make, and then I didn't have to have quite as many customers as usual. Then, I could go home and thus avoid some of the worst and most drunken customers at the end of the night, when it was often the worst.

But it was mostly in the beginning when I still had some inhibitions and hadn't become so hard-skinned. At that time, I still had a bit of a hard time with those who were too drunk or disgusting.

But by now, I had been at it for a few years and had gotten used to it a little more. I already had about fifteen names in different places on my body, so I thought that might be enough. I didn't want to look too totally cheap and trashy. However, there are quite a few men who are turned on by this kind of thing, so it can give some extra customers. So that it's me that they will choose over one of the other girls. But there is still a limit one somewhere. And now I had at least decided to stop doing that part of the business and had held on to my decision for quite a while. Almost half a year, I think it was.

But that guy wasn't easy to get rid of again. He kept insisting. It was probably also because he could see all the names of men that I already had tattooed on me. So even though I had stopped doing this kind of thing, I still gave in in the end, just to get rid of him. There was nothing else to do. After all, one more didn't mean much. But in return, I demanded triple the price of what I used to charge for it. Just to test him. But he paid what I demanded without further ado.

But when we got to the tattoo shop, he was unstoppable. Then he wanted something more tattooed on me. And he would pay me good money for it. And now I was just getting started, so the easiest thing was to just keep going. I was, after all I was not completely very sober at the time. That was probably a little why. But I was smart enough to still demand triple payment. But that didn't deter him. I think he'd just made a fortune or something like that.

Then, I might as well take advantage of it. I had seen a big design that I would like to have made. So why not get him to pay the tattoo artist to make it on me and then give me money on top of that for a great design that I had wanted for some time?

And he was totally on board with that. The tattoo artist went to work. He could only just make the outline for it now because there were a lot of details. And then I agreed with the guy that he would come back in a few days, and then I would have it finished. But I probably shouldn't have done that. I figured he'd forgotten about it again, so I didn't see him anymore. But he showed up one of the days between Christmas and New Year's Eve, and then it turned out a little differently from what I thought.

But that's a whole other story. I must stick to all that stuff about Connie and Jansen and what I was doing in the meantime, just to explain why I didn't get to Connie in her apartment until much later than I had planned. It was already past midnight when I finally got there, and then I had missed a whole lot of what had happened in the meantime.

We had arranged to meet for a goodnight beer at Cap Horn at eleven and a half o'clock, that is, Connie and I and him, the filmmaker, because Connie wanted to introduce me to him too because maybe there was a role for me in that movie adventure as well.

At least she said afterward that this was what they had been talking about. But they had been sitting there waiting in vain for me while I got that all ink done. And in the end, they had gotten a little angry at me because they had been waiting for me when I didn't come anyway, and then they went to her place.

When I had finally been half-decorated some more, I mean it hadn't been finished at all, I hurried to her place all I could, but by then, it had already become almost half past one o'clock.

They were still a little mad at me. They couldn't understand where I had been. It took some time for me to explain. After all, none of us were very sober at the time.

But gradually, we thawed out a little, and Connie told me about some of what that filmmaker had offered her. It was amazing. Almost like she was going to be a big movie star. After all, she had the looks for it. Then he started talking about the offer he had for me, too, and then I pricked up my ears.

But he didn't even get to finish talking about it because suddenly Jansen came bursting in and disturbed everything, just at the wrong moment. He came in as if he owned it all and shouted, "Who is that man?" in a very aggressive voice, pointing his finger at the filmmaker who was sitting peacefully in a chair.

The filmmaker wondered what was going on, but he quickly perceived the hostile tone and attitude of Jansen.

It turned out that there were some pretty hefty rumors circulating about Connie and the filmmaker and his golden promises to her. Apparently, it had run around the entire environment, and of course, those rumors have also reached the basement tavern where Jansen was. And he maybe assumed that Connie would disappear from his life if she were to become a movie star. And then he became completely obsessed with jealousy of that filmmaker and mad at him. All evening, he had been drinking heavily, so he was more drunk than usual when he tumbled into Connie's house, where she and I sat quietly and chatted with the filmmaker.

Jansen hurled the worst invective he could while the filmmaker tried to calm him down, though he didn't quite understand why Jansen was so furious. He didn't know anything about his entire backstory with Connie. But he did what he could to pour some oil on the waters.

It just didn't help anything. And some of what he said excited Jansen even more. Jansen took a large ceramic dish and wanted to smash it into the head of the filmmaker, who was still sitting down. Fortunately, he managed to turn to the side to avoid being hit. And then he stood up and hurried to take shelter next to a closet in the corner of the living room. He couldn't get to the door because Jansen was standing in the way.

But now Jansen took a chair, which he held up and wanted to smash into his head. The filmmaker yelled at him to stop and a whole lot more. Meanwhile, I managed to kick Jansen in the kneecaps from behind, causing him to lose his footing and sink to the floor, aching heavily. The filmmaker seized the opportunity and fled out the door and into the street as fast as he could, and none of us had seen anything of him since.

In Connie's living room, Jansen had collapsed like a rag doll and had thrown up all over the carpet and everything. Soon after, he began to cry like a child. He just stayed there and kept crying for a long time, completely inconsolable.

Then he made all sorts of reproaches and scolded god and every man, but gradually mostly himself and threatened to go out and do an accident to himself. And I don't think it was just an empty threat. It sounded like he meant it.

Eventually, he got up and staggered a little to find his balance. Then he slowly started walking toward the door and said he was going to go out and jump into the canal and kill himself.

But then Connie took pity on him and tried to persuade him not to do so and rather stay with her for the night. But he still wanted to do it, he said and started walking toward the door again.

But now Connie held him back by force. It was a lot easier because he was dead drunk and couldn't fight back. Together, we managed to tie him to an armchair so he could hardly move and could not leave the apartment. Or so we thought. And we poured some beer with a couple of aspirins into him to get him to calm down and preferably sleep. But it took a while before it was working, and now he started talking again about jumping into the canal and putting an end to it all.

When he tried to get up from the chair and maybe would try to walk away with the chair still bound onto his body, Connie hurried to sit down on his lap to hold him down, so he stayed in the chair until the pills started working while she talked a lot of reassuring talk to him. A few times during the first few minutes, he tried to get up again, so I had to help Connie hold him down so that he stayed put. Fortunately, it wasn't that long before the aspirins started working. In addition to that, he also had quite a lot to drink during the evening. In a short time, he seemed to be sleeping soundly and snoring loudly.

But we were afraid that he would wake up during the night while we were sleeping and then run away and jump in the canal to drown himself. After all, it was just outside, on the other side of the street.

We didn't really know how many if those aspirins would be safe to give him and how long the effect lasted. When he started dozing off, we took a sheet of bed linen and tore it into some wide strips, and then we simply tied him once more to the armchair he was sleeping in and then tied the armchair to a big heavy table. We wanted to be sure he didn't come up with anything stupid during the night. Then he could sit there and sleep it off and hopefully look at it a little differently when he got sober.

That was the only thing we could think of. And then we both went to bed, both Connie and I, because we were both really tired and drunk and needed a lot of sleep ourselves.

The Golden Bikini

Connie, of course, was very disappointed that the filmmaker had disappeared. After all, she was beginning to dream about all that stuff about becoming a movie star. All that he had promised her. But now it didn't come to anything. She tried to find him. But he had already left the hotel. I think he had traveled on. She didn't know much about him either, like his address or telephone number, for example. She never found him. Back then, you couldn't just Google him and find out everything about him. It was way back in 1970, this happened. All that stuff about the internet hadn't even been invented yet. She just had to give it up. She also didn't know anyone in the film industry she could ask. But she was very disappointed that it didn't happen anyway. And it was also suggested that I might be able to join it. We talked a lot about it. All that stuff with Jansen had taken a toll on her as well. She wasn't feeling very well.

Once, in the early summer of the following year, she met a young guy who wanted to make a movie. Just as an amateur. Not one of the established ones. He said he was a film student. And not one that was in the film industry as such. Just a young guy who dreamed of becoming a film director and went around and filmed everything with a small camera. A 16mm camera, he said. Not a real movie camera. And then it turned out that this guy named Paul wanted to make a movie with Connie and me. It was not very good what came out of it. But it was a lot of fun.

It was meant to be a road movie where Connie and I drive off in a car, and then you follow our drive and what we experience along the way. First, we had to get a car to drive. One we could borrow. It wasn't that easy at all. No one wanted to lend their car to Connie and me. After all, she didn't have a car herself. I did not, either. Neither did Paul. I don't know if that's why. Or maybe people were afraid we were drunk and would smash the car or something. Paul ended up borrowing his parents' car. It was an old SAAB. With a two-stroke engine. The kind that makes farting noises when the engine idles. Paul had thought that it was a big car we were going to drive, with that great engine sound from a V8 engine, but now it became an old SAAB instead. Connie and I had to sit in front, Connie had to be the driver, and I had to sit next to her, and then Paul sat in the back seat with his little film camera and some sound equipment and recorded what happened along the way. There was no film crew, only Paul, Connie and me. Keep it simple, sweetheart. That's a well-known saying in the film industry. Only Paul exaggerated it. But it just had to be tried.

    He just shot the whole drive, filming through the windshield and so that the picture would show a bit of Connie and me seen from behind, and everything Connie and I talked about was recorded, as well as the sound of the two-stroke engine. It wasn't like we had to learn some lines we should say. There was no real script, just some ideas that he had jotted down on a piece of paper. The idea was just to take a trip out into the summer country, drive all the way to the beach, with two beautiful girls like Connie and me, and then he figured that something probably happened along the way that could be made into a movie when you cut it together in the right way afterward.

    Paul recorded it all. The road we drove on, filmed out through the windshield, and everything Connie and I talked about along the way. In the beginning, it was a bit difficult to just talk plainly and spontaneously when you knew it was all being recorded. But we forgot rather quickly, and then we talked about all sorts of things as usual. Including a lot of nonsense and some things that were a bit embarrassing. Because we forgot it was recorded. Paul just sat quietly in the back and filmed and recorded it all without saying a word. He did not interfere at all. I once watched the whole raw film with Connie when Paul showed it to us. It was far too long for a regular movie. After all, it was the whole drive. It lasted about eight hours. And most of the time not much happened. Except for all the nonsense that Connie and I were firing off. Paul had said that we should talk about some of the customers we had had and, of course, especially those who had been the worst, or the most special, and so on. And there was plenty to talk about there, so we got a little carried away by it and got a little nonsensical at the end and exaggerated some of it quite a lot. Some of it has become quite entertaining to listen to. And all the time, there was that engine sound from the two-stroke engine in the background.

At some point, we had to stop at a supermarket to do some shopping for the picnic.

A number of men were glancing at us and making naughty remarks, but we brushed them off with some humorous remarks so that the men became the laughing stock instead. They don't even know they're in our movie.

We laughed about that as we drove on. A little later, we stopped at a gas station to fill up the tank. Connie went to the kiosk while I refuel. But I must first drive the car to the stand with moped gas because the car must have oil in the gasoline because it is a two-stroke. Paul is still filming it all. Now, it's the gas station where there are quite a lot of people swarming around.

Then I went to the kiosk to pay. There was someone on the other end of the square shouting loudly, but it was probably not something that concerned me, so I just rushed to the kiosk. I went inside and had to wait a bit to pay because there were a few others in front of me. Connie was still standing at the other end of the kiosk and had a hard time choosing what to buy.

I made my pay and rushed out. Just outside was someone I knew. That was not very good. Because it was a guy named Brian, and he was one of those people who'd come to my love nest in the backyard a couple of times. He is the only one of them who had been troublesome. And rather much so.

Now, he was standing there a little further on, grabbing me. I got loose and hurried on. But now Connie had come out of the kiosk, and he grabbed her and was going to drag her along.

Oh my god, this was really bad, I thought. I turned around and ran back to Brian and unloaded him in the crotch, so he curled up, and the well-aimed kick with one of my boots made him let go of Connie, and he just stood there aching in pain. Two of his friends came up to him from the big Buick, which was further along, engine running and everything.

Connie and I ran as fast as we could to the old SAAB. And now it's great that we left it with the engine running. I was in front, so I jumped behind the wheel. Connie was right behind; she jumped into the front seat on the other side. We hammered the doors shut, I slammed the steering wheel gear up into the first gear and twisted the car around in a kind of slalom to get out of the gas station and get around a few other cars that were in our way, and around a nearly ninety-degree corner to get out on the road, where I just managed to slip in front of a Plymouth.

Finally, I shifted into the second gear, which the engine had long sounded like it wanted me to.

As always, Paul just sat in the back seat and filmed it all, calm and unchallenged. That man must have nerves of steel, I thought. But this was obviously his view of what a real cinematographer should be like, no matter what happened around him. After all, the film had gone completely off the track compared to what was planned. All these things just happened, much to our own surprise. The guys in the black Buick were chasing us and trying to catch up with us. But Paul just kept filming it all.

I tried to slip away from them. It developed into a car chase along small secondary roads and forest roads. The small roads suited the SAAB just fine. I drove it as hard as I could and twisted it around the bends on the small, winding roads. The SAAB was better at this than the big Buick.

At one point, we drove for some time through a big forest. We drove along some small gravel roads, and suddenly, we came to a stream, which we had to cross on a small narrow wooden bridge. It was not meant for cars at all, but it was wide enough for the old SAAB but far too narrow for the big Buick. In this way, we managed to get away from them.

As it happened, it got much more dramatic than planned. Paul was smart enough to turn the camera around and move to one corner of the back seat so that the camera filmed out the rear window, so you could see the big Buick pursuing us, at least when it was close. But when we saw the film, it almost made you seasick, because the camera swung around quickly with the car in the narrow turns, while the road was rather bumpy, so the camera was shaking quite a bit.

But what luck that we managed to get away from the rough guys in the Buick. Now Paul thought we should return to his script, which was just very sketchy. Nothing at all with lines or anything like that. Picnic in a forest by the beach. He had found out in advance exactly where. That was very important, he said. It had to be there and nowhere else.

It took at least half an hour to get there. It is pretty boring in the long version of the film—the unedited one—although he continued to film out the back window to suggest that we're probably still being chased by the big Buick, so it might reappear in a short time, even though Connie and I had just been talking about how nice it was, that we got rid of them.

But it might be that we were wrong about it and that they were still pursuing us and would suddenly appear behind us, the spectators are supposed to think, so as to create some tension in this rather monotonous part of the film.

At one point, a Volkswagen appeared behind us for a long while, so maybe the spectators thought it was a new phase of the car chase…

Finally, we got to where we were supposed to have a picnic. After all, we had food and drinks with us. We found a place where we could sit on a blanket in the grass and have a very delayed lunch. Now Paul had finally gotten out of the car to film our picnic. He had put his film camera on a tripod, so it filmed Connie and me going for a picnic while he sat on a folding chair behind the camera and ate his food. After all, he was the cinematographer and was not supposed to be in the film. He strictly held on to that.

And then it was time for the golden bikinis. Which was to be the title of the film. It was completely silly. It was meant as an advertisement for those bikinis and the company that sold them. They were made of some
golden fabric and were quite small. But both the bra cups and the panties were equipped with a tiny kind of skirt. It was made

of some silver fabric, obviously contrasting with the golden one. But we didn't know all that yet. Now, we had to find them first.

We were going around looking for them in the woods. Like some kind of a treasure hunt. Pretty silly. We had to go around looking for them and had to look everywhere. Fortunately, they were not that hard to find. First, Connie found one in a dense stand of some large ferns. Soon after, I found one in a hollow tree. Once we had found them, we had to hold them up so that the camera could make a close-up of the packaging so you could see the logo and company name.

When we unpacked them, it turned out that they were not the same. Connie's was the one I described just before. Mine was reversed in terms of gold and silver. But it could be just as good for that reason, I thought.

But no, it couldn't anyway. For now, Connie and I had to pretend to get into a fight over who should get which one of the golden bikinis—the original or the opposite. It was something that a marketing guy had come up with. For some reason, we both wanted the original one. That meant that I was going to try to conquer it from Connie, who also wanted it and absolutely wouldn't give it up. Connie and I had to fight over it corporally. It was supposed to be like a catfight where two furious women rip each other's clothes off. We had both been told to put on a blouse and miniskirt throughout the trip.

The one of us who first had all the clothes ripped off the other so that she stood completely naked was the one that had won and thus had gained the right to the original golden bikini, while the other had to make do with the reverse. It was Connie who won, and now I was standing there, stark naked. This was probably meant to be the picture of the movie poster. It annoyed me a little that my tattooist had recently left for a study trip in Japan and had canceled the agreement to put the missing colors on the rest of the big dragon tattoo that was made at Christmas time, so it still wasn't finished.

Connie had also taken off the last bit of clothing, and so we stood there, naked, next to each other, putting on our golden bikinis. It was summer and hot weather, so that was the only thing we should wear, plus gold sandals on our feet. Then we had to sit on the lunch blanket in the grass and drink a Coke, each eagerly talking about how lucky we had been to find those gold bikinis, so now there was probably a golden future ahead.

The next thing we had been instructed to do was that we suddenly had to find some dollar bills in a small pocket inside one of the bra cups. First Connie, then me. A neat little pile of banknotes. This was because the company that sold them had created a competition where you could win some cash prizes, which were raffled off among everyone who bought one of the amazing golden bikinis. But I didn't really know how it was shown in the movie. It could perhaps be misunderstood.

But then something new had to happen in the film. And that was an angry farmer with a shotgun that came running toward us, shouting and screaming about the immorality of the time and the lack of decency of today's youth while he aimed at us with his shotgun to chase us away, for it was his grass in his wood where we sat, and nobody was allowed to be sitting on his property in a bikini, and certainly not such a naughty and daring golden one, that he thought was one of the most obvious signs of the decay of morality and the unbridled youth of modern times.

We got a little scared until we realized that it was planned as part of the action. The angry old farmer's outrage at today's youth who wore golden bikinis was apparently supposed to be promotional and make it even more trendy among young girls to have one.

It turned out that the farmer was Paul's uncle, and we found out that actually he was a farmer and had a small farm up here on the coast. That's why this was the place where we were going to have the picnic.

But now another person came onto the scene. It was a very heavily bleached blonde who, on the other hand, was incredibly tanned. Her name was Betsy, and even though she was no longer young, she was still a few years younger than Paul's uncle, whom she was married to, it turned out. It was she who ran the company that imported the golden bikinis from somewhere abroad. However, she herself was quite commonly dressed in a summer dress. She seemed nice and easy-going. She told us a little about her company and how she herself had gotten to know the golden bikinis.

But then suddenly something happened again. The guys in the black Buick had apparently found out where we were anyway, and suddenly, they came driving along a small dirt road. And this was not part of the planned action. But now the uncle acted quickly. With his shotgun, he fired a shot right over the roof of the Buick and shouted in an angry voice that they should disappear. When they did not react, he fired again and planted a shot in two tree trunks, one on each side of the road, right next to the car, and that made them hurry to get away. It was included in the film, along with a speaker's comment that it was because they wanted to steal the golden bikinis, but of course, it wasn't.

Now, it was getting late in the evening, and there was a beautiful sunset on this summer's day. Now Connie and I were instructed to go down to the beach, which was nearby, still wearing nothing but our golden bikinis, and then we had to embrace each other on the shore with the sunset as a background.

We kissed each other—for the first time ever—and as proof of her great love for me, Connie had to say that she would exchange the golden bikini with me and give me hers, the original, which for some reason should be much better than the other one, that I was wearing. It was in the script, so of course, we did as we were instructed. So now there would be another long nude scene, this time at the beach with the sunset over the sea in the background. It was probably much longer than planned because when Connie and I first got to kiss and hug each other for the second time, we could hardly let go of each other again. But then we swapped the bikinis as we were told. The film ends with Connie and me, hand in hand, walking slowly along the shoreline with the sea to the left and a stunningly beautiful sunset sky in the most amazing colors.

Paul did finish the film and had it cut down to the length of an ordinary movie, but it never made it to the movie theaters the way it was meant to. It was probably too primitively made. Some of it seems very crazy. He showed it to Connie and me. There is plenty of poor sound and image quality. And long scenes with not much action. Perhaps the nude scenes were also too much for film censorship at the time. It was way back in 1970. Perhaps it was extra provocative to the self-appointed moral guardians that it is two women who are kissing and hugging so fiercely in the final scene, and not a man and a woman.

Connie's Baby

It wasn't long after her breakup with Jansen at Christmas that Connie told me she was pregnant and that she wanted the baby. You couldn't see it on her yet, but it wasn't long before it started to become apparent. As I said, it was right after her long affair with Jansen, so it may well be that he was the father. But I don't know. Connie herself always used to say that she was sure that it was he who was the father of the child she was expecting. Why she was so sure of that, I don't know. I mean, with all the men she was with every single day. But maybe because she only had unprotected sex with him. Otherwise, she was always very careful about this kind of thing. Maybe she would like to have his child.

At least she insisted that she wanted the baby. And apparently, it was not a matter of course that she could just decide for herself. Her parents over in Jutland and her aunt pressed hard for the child to be adopted. But she wouldn't. Absolutely not. She wanted to keep her baby. She was fully prepared to do so. It wasn't so ordinary then. In 1970, it was still not widely accepted. Many still considered it almost shameful to have a child out of wedlock and even with a random acquaintance.

But Connie's parents and her aunt insisted that the baby should be adopted immediately after birth. This was often used at the time in such situations. Apparently, one did not think about the psychological and other problems it could cause for both mother and child, but only about whether it was 'nice' and 'respectable' based on the strict and oppressive morals of the time.

But Connie wouldn't give up her baby. She didn't want it to be put up for adoption. She wanted to keep her baby herself. She kept repeating this throughout her pregnancy. And I think she would have become a really good and caring mother if only she had been allowed to.

But she wasn't.

Someone else decided that over her head. In full agreement with the doctors and midwives in the maternity clinic and the entire official system. That was often the case back then.

It was a private maternity clinic that her aunt knew and had Connie admitted to when she was due to give birth. Such maternity clinics were quite common back then. It was pre-arranged (with everyone but Connie herself) and arranged so that the baby was taken from her shortly after birth and cared for by a midwife or a nursing assistant until the adoptive parents could come and pick up the baby as soon as possible. Connie's baby.

The birth had started a few days before she was due, and apparently, the adoptive parents were not properly prepared for that, so it took a few extra days before the adoptive parents arrived from a city far away to pick up the baby.

I just couldn't bear to watch how hard it was taking on Connie. And that's when I did something that I probably shouldn't have done. It was no use anyway. But it was done with the best of intentions. I didn't know what else to do. I couldn't just let it happen.

I had prepared it all very thoroughly. It wasn't just a random whim. It was carefully planned. I had bought or purchased all the necessary baby equipment and asked someone I knew who had two children, aged one and three, for advice on everything I could think of. I had also provided an apartment where Connie could be with her child at an address you didn't have to give to the national register, so they couldn't just go out and find us. It was a small apartment inside a backyard. But there was what was supposed to be, even if it was small and looked pretty run down. And the owner was not one to gossip about who lived there. Although, in some ways, he was a bit of a jerk—or maybe that's why. He was not the type to approach the authorities about anything.

It was the very same apartment that I had used a few years ago as a meeting place—or probably more correctly said—as a hut for the men that I had to take care of and be a little nice to. My old pink love nest. I had long since moved out. Now, it had been standing empty for a while, so he was perfectly willing to rent it out to me again. On more common terms this time, that is, without men who came running and had to be serviced. I had conditioned myself to do so. The only consideration—apart from the rent—was that once a week, I would come to him where he was staying and be kind and loving to him and maybe a few of his guests. After all, it was manageable. I was already in the profession, and I did it for Connie's sake. For Connie and her baby.

I visited Connie at the maternity clinic a few hours after she had given birth. The baby had already been taken away from her and put into a room where it was cared for by a midwife. Or maybe it was a nanny. One of the staff at the clinic. They thought that the child would attach itself to the adoptive parents when it had not managed to gain any attachment to its own biological mother.

After talking to Connie and trying to comfort her as best I could, I went into action. Connie was obviously privy to the plan, but we made sure not to talk too loudly about it.

I had prepared it all thoroughly in advance. I had somehow mysteriously gotten myself a nurse's uniform that I had borrowed from someone I knew a little. I went to the bathroom and changed my clothes so I looked like one of the nurses.

I discreetly watched the room where Connie's child had been placed, and when the child slept soundly and the one who looked after it left the room because she was called to the phone in the guard room next door, I saw my chance to snatch the baby—a little girl who was still sleeping soundly—out of the cradle and hide her in a big bag with a soft pillow, which I had carried in a backpack.

And then out the door and away from the maternity clinic with the baby as soon as possible, out into the street and hailing a taxi, and then to the small apartment in the back yard, where I had everything ready for a baby and had made an appointment with Kirsten, whom I knew from my time at the university, and who had two children herself, to assist us.

It took two days before Connie was discharged from the maternity clinic. There had been a lot of confusion about what had happened to the child, but they probably thought that it was the adoptive parents who had been there and picked it up without it having been registered properly, as it should, and apparently, they could not get in touch with them. It was our luck.

So now we were almost a whole little family in the pink brothel apartment. Connie and I all the time, and Kirsten a lot of the time to share her experience with us. And Connie's little girl, who I will always know again because she had a rather large birthmark on the left arm slightly above the elbow and a slightly smaller one almost in the same place on the right arm. Almost symmetrical. It was probably a slightly bigger task than I had thought, and Connie was just starting out as a mother. But there is no doubt that she really loved that child. It simply shone out of her, so she wouldn't even have been able to hide it if she wanted to. And we got a good help from Kirsten. It was tremendously nicely done by her.

I had dropped my other activities and was there all the time.

But the joy lasted only briefly. After only a few weeks, they had found the place, which was not officially registered as an apartment anywhere. And, of course, they had long since gotten into trouble with the planned adoptive parents, who accused them of sloppiness when the child could just disappear like that.

And then it turned out the way they had always wanted it to be. Despite all of Connie's protests and her arguing that since her child had already bonded with her during the first few weeks, it was probably the best thing for the child to stay with her. She tried to use their own arguments against them. But it was no use. They must have had hearts of stone.

Connie's baby was given up for adoption anyway, just as it had been planned all along. There was nothing to do. The machine of bureaucracy ran relentlessly and was unstoppable once it was set in motion.

Connie has never seen her child again after the day they came to pick it up. She doesn't even know where the family lives, other than that it is in a city far away in another state. She doesn't know their names or what they are like. What things in life do they value the most? She doesn't even know what name they gave her, little girl.

That's what knocked Connie out. That they took her child away from her, and it was after that time that she started drinking hard and didn't care about herself and what she was getting herself into. That's when she really broke down. OK, there was probably already something broken in her that infamous evening with all those drunken sailors. But not nearly as much as now. At that time, she was not a drunkard; she did not skimp on things, and she took care of herself. She looked terrific; she had her radiant smile and could be very charming even though many may have considered her a cheap hooker even then because of what she was doing.

But now, after this, it was all gone, her self-respect and her charm, and she didn't care for herself any more. Of course, there were also the other disappointments. All that with the office manager. Jansen and all the filmmaker's golden promises that came to nothing. Of course, it's also a hard life in general. But not nearly as much as when they took her child away from her. That is what made the biggest difference.

As far as I'm concerned, they dragged me to court for stealing Connie's child. I don't know if they ever understood what the context really was. But at least I went to court and had to be convicted of it as an offense. The prosecutor wanted me sentenced to six months in prison. It was a female judge. I don't know if she understood me, maybe a little bit, but she was content to suspend the sentence, but still six months. But I didn't have to go to jail.

Of course, looking back on it, it was a stupid thing to do. There was no point in wanting to change what the system had decided, no matter how unreasonable it was. And it was ravingly naïve to think that you could get away with it, no matter how carefully you had planned everything. But heck, it was an act out of sheer desperation.

My Re-Education

Once again, I was in trouble. This time, too, someone was trying to get me on an even keel. At least, that's what they called it. But at the time, I didn't look at it that way myself. I was quite averse to it and even tried to fight back. But, of course, it was no use.

So now it had turned out that way anyway. And then I had to try to make the best of it. I had been sent to the countryside so that I could get out into the fresh air and the beautiful green nature. And above all, away from the noise and fuss of the big city. Far away from everything.

I almost felt like I had been deported to Siberia or something like that. I had gone into foster care. The word itself sounded quite degrading, I thought. As something for orphans. Not because there is anything wrong with orphans. Not at all. But I was an adult and twenty-five years old! I wasn't a kid any more. I probably had far more experience with several things than the two persons in the oh-so-nice foster family would probably ever have. But that was probably precisely the problem. I had too much experience with the wrong things—in their opinion, the system, the social services, the caseworkers. Even if it wasn't crime or drugs, I'd been on. But there were many other things that were wrong in their opinion. I was a little too fond of men, they said. I guess it was just because the men were a little too fond of me, and then I gave them back in the same way. But the social workers didn't understand something like that.

As I said, it was out in the countryside, that place where they had put me. It was in the middle of nowhere. The people I was going to live with were a middle-aged couple whose children had grown up and left home and probably were college students. I only met them once.

The wife in the house was trained as a social worker or something, but now she was at home and took care of both the household and the young girls they had in care. They had had a whole row of them before me. But only one at a time. In addition, she was responsible for the small business with used furniture and antiques, which they sold from what had been the barn when the place was a farm. Not a big farm, just a small homestead. But I think that was a long time ago.

The man she was married to was the chief accountant of some company in a town many miles from there. He drove off in the car every morning. And then it was only Lizzie, as the wife was called, and me. In the beginning, she got on my nerves. She was a completely different type than me. It was a completely different environment than I was used to. Another world, almost. It took a while before we got on speaking terms.

Part of my re-education to a 'nice girl' or a 'nice and sensible girl,' as it was called——was that I had to learn something about household chores. For example, I learned to cook as a real housewife did, where it all had to be made from scratch instead of making it a little easy.

Or something like learning how to set a nice table for guests. If it was a small family celebration. Or a larger family party. There is a difference between that, I can tell you. You have no idea how many things that need to be done in a certain way for it to be a successful (family) party. According to Lizzie, Mrs. Super-Housewife. For example, did you know that it really matters how you fold the napkins? And that there are so many ways to fold a napkin? Of course, it is the most intricate and complicated ones that give the best forecast for a successful family celebration. According to Lizzie.

Fortunately, I didn't have to learn them all. Only ten or twelve of them. Approximately. These were the kind of people where you had to hold your tongue. Mrs. Super-Housewife knew so much about folding napkins, and she generously shared her knowledge more than generously even. Apparently, it was something that could really put her in the mood for a party if the napkins were folded in just the right way.

But of course, these were only the more exotic parts of housewifery. Most of it was much more mundane. Cooking I have already mentioned. It took up a lot of time to learn to cook like a housewife. Then there was the daily cleaning. Vacuuming, washing the floor, wiping off dust, arranging showers and toilets, cleaning the kitchen so that it shone.

And the laundry. It was incredible how carefully the laundry had to be sorted out. I also had to learn how to iron shirts and other clothes. But mostly shirts. Her husband's shirts. His name was Eric. I think I haven't mentioned that before. He had to wear a clean, freshly washed, and freshly ironed shirt every morning when he left for the office. It quickly became one of my daily tasks. I'll say no more about that. Otherwise, I didn't have much to do with him, even though he was often home on weekends when he wasn't at a meeting or convention of some kind. He quite often was.

And that was a good thing. I was perfectly fine with that.

I also had to learn how to keep household accounts. All expenses had to be carefully written into a small accounting book with printed columns for the numbers. And then the expenses had to be counted together, and you finally had to make sure that it was exactly right on dollars and cents. I've never been very good at something like that.

I also had to help with the furniture in the old barn. There was a lot of old furniture. They had to be refurbished and perhaps painted, but mostly deacidified. Most were in an old-fashioned style. These were some furniture that they bought around from old people on the farms and small villages nearby. Then, they put them in good condition and sold them to wealthy city dwellers. Apparently, some people thought it was very smart or romantic or something with that kind of old authentic furniture from the countryside.

There was quite a lot of work involved with that furniture. They usually had to be restored and fixed up and everything. But now they had me as free labor without a paycheck. A big part of my day, I was supposed to be working with that.

I also had to go to the grocery store. There was a small local grocery store not too far away in what they called the village. But it was just a small collection of houses and a few old farms, about fifteen in all. But there was also a grocery store. It was only a quarter of an hour's walk from where they lived.

There was no supermarket nearby. There weren't any other shops either. Only that little grocery store. He, the old grocer, on the other hand, had a little bit of everything in his shop.

There was also no bakery nearby. They baked all their bread themselves. Or, that is, she did. Eric hardly ever set foot in the kitchen at all. I also had to learn to bake bread. I wasn't exactly used to that either.

There was also no butcher shop. The grocery shop did not sell meat. Only if it was canned, everything they needed of this kind was delivered from a refrigerated truck that came there every two weeks and unloaded a lot of deep-frozen meat products that they had ordered from a list to fill out. All that meat then had to be put in the right place in the two large freezers in the utility room.

It became my job to go to the grocery store. One of my regular daily duties. Because almost every day, there was something to be picked up at the grocery store. Coffee, tea, sugar, a bag of flour, a can of peas, a bag of carrots. Anything.

Lizzie had also got the idea that someone like me probably needed a lot of healthy exercise out in the fresh air. So, on my daily trip to the grocery store for various small things—or maybe a little more—I also had to go for an extra run, just an hour and a half, kind of around the beautiful little roads between the lush green fields with the grazing cows and the grain that matured in the most beautiful summer wind.

In the Back Room of the Grocery Store

And I did, dutifully as I should. In the beginning, at least. Because it turned out that there was a little more going on in the grocery store than you might have thought. There were often some men playing cards in the back room. Some of the old or half-old men who had nothing else to do. Then they sat there and beat up the old, greasy playing cards while drinking beer. Sometimes, the merchant's wife came in with a platter of open sandwiches, which they had to pay for. After lunch, they had coffee. It was always his wife that served the food, the coffee, and the beers.

When she bent over the table to serve food or pour coffee, or to clean off the table, she bent down further than was necessary so that one of her large, flaccid hanging breasts fell out of the neckline of her blouse and hung there dangling out in the open right in front of one of the men. Then he put a few coins for her as a tip. But only if she did it like that. It was disgusting.

Once she had cleared off, poured them coffee, and placed a new bottle of beer in front of each of them, they picked up the cards again and played on. Sometimes, the merchant also played along when there were no customers in the store. There was a bell above the shop door that rang when someone opened the door and entered the shop. Then, he had to rush to the store to process them. But it wasn't until a little later that I realized all that was going on.

The merchant had quickly looked me out and seen what I

was. That day, I had been out for an hour because now I wanted to show my goodwill to be the 'sweet and sensible girl' that they wanted me to be.

That special day, I had been obediently and patiently running around the small secondary roads for an hour. It was a day in mid-May, and it had become glorious sunshine and a really hot summer's day, so I was both thirsty and sweaty after the run when I finally stepped inside the grocery store to buy the things I was told to buy—complete with a shopping list and all. But the merchant knew what I was. He probably also knew very well that these were the kind of girls—or young women—that Lizzie and Eric used to have living with them. Everyone there probably knew that. I wasn't the first one of my kind. I guess that he immediately saw some possibilities.

As he gazed at my T-shirt, which was soaked in sweat and therefore clung to my breasts, he said nicely and kindly that I looked like I had been out for a run in the heat and if I might be thirsty after the run.

Because then he would like to offer me a beer. At the house's expense, of course. I was thirsty, so I said a Coca-Cola would be fine.

But I could also have a beer if I preferred that, he said. How about a nice cold beer? Was that something? You can get the one you like best. It's entirely up to you, he said.

But I maintained that I wanted a Coke.

Then I'm going to go and fetch it in the back room, he said. But you can come along yourself. Then you can also get a chair to sit on while you enjoy it. We are generous people here, you know.

It was the first time I was in the back room. I probably shouldn't have agreed to go in there. But I did.

When I got there, there were four elderly men sitting at a table playing cards. All four of them immediately looked up from the card game and at me and my rather sweat-soaked T-shirt.

One of the men took out his wallet and put some money on the table.

"To you," he said. "If you come closer and take off your blouse in front of us. Just pull it over your head so we can see what you have got."

I was speechless. Even with my background and my past, I was a little flabbergasted. I've tried a little bit of everything when it comes to cranky, disgusting men in my profession. But I wasn't at work now. Or was it the first few months of re-socialization that had already brought me out of training to deal with this kind of thing?

I shook my head. Then, I took a hold of myself. I looked him directly in the eye and said loud and clear, "No."

Now, the merchant came up to me and said, "You better take off the wet T-shirt. Otherwise, you will catch a cold."

Then he shouted in a commanding voice that would probably have done well at the Army recruit school.

"Marie, go fetch a blouse for Yvonne."

I hadn't told him my name, even though I had been to the store quite a few times, but always only out front, in the store itself. But everyone in the area probably knew my name and why I lived with Lizzie and Eric—from the usual gossip, simply.

A moment later, his wife entered through the door at the back of the room. Her name was Marie. She was a slightly heavily built woman of about fifty. She had a bit of the same charisma as an obedient and well-behaved dog.

She fetched a blouse for me. To put on instead of the T-shirt. It was a red shirt blouse with a lot of ruffles on it. Not exactly my style.

"You can come in here and change," she said and showed me a corner behind some beer crates and a bunch of stacked cardboard cartons of various grocery items. I went there and changed. That was it. And then I hurried out and away from there. But I should also buy the groceries that were on my list and which were what I had come for. I told the merchant. The four card players looked completely disappointed that I left their little drunkard bulge so quickly. But that was fine with me. I took the bottle of Coke with me.

"I'll drink it on the way," I said. "I'd better hurry back so Lizzie doesn't worry about me."

"As you prefer," he said. "You must apologize to those four men in the back room. They can be a little direct in their manner sometimes. But once you get to know them, they are nice guys."

"It was those groceries," I said, handing him Lizzie's list. I got the items I needed and put them in the shopping bag along with the sweat-soaked T-shirt.

"You can keep the red blouse," he said. "It's a gift from me to you. But remember to put it on the next time you come here."

WHAT? I wanted to yell, but instead, I just rushed out the shop door and started my little walk home to Lizzie-house.

When I was almost home, (yes, I had started calling it that!) I went behind a couple of trees and some bushes by the side of the road and changed. I put the red blouse in the bag. Then I fished out the T-shirt and put it on, even though it was both wet and clammy. But for some reason, I didn't want Lizzie to see me in the red ruffle thing. Not right now, at least. Then there would just be something I had to explain.

The next day, I was at the grocery store again. And in the back room, along with those card players. Sometimes, they even played about me. Then I had to go to the back room with the winner of the card game and satisfy him in the way he told me. I don't know why I kept coming back there. They even paid me money. I guess I could have just said no. But I didn't. I kept going there all summer, every day. Gradually, there was not much running around on the country roads. I went straight to the grocery store and into the back room with the card players and made a lot of money. And then a quick run at high speed back home with the groceries after what eventually turned into a few hours. The rest of the time, I was in the back room. It's hard to explain why. Perhaps it was a kind of rebelliousness toward Lizzie. And all the nice bourgeois kind of behavior she wanted me to get into. Or an attempt to see how far I could go before she said stop. To see how much I could get away with. But she never realized it. Although it sounds incredible. Everyone in the community must have known what was going on at the grocery store, admittedly in the back room and only to a small circle of disgusting old men who apparently had nothing else to do. They probably expected that the young girls from Lizzie-House would sooner or later show up at their back room, where they sat and beat the cards and drank beers most of the day. With the poor wife of the merchant to serve them beer and food and whatever. It was a real shame for her. She seemed very suppressed. Perhaps she had been so suppressed for many years that she was no longer able to break out of what, by all accounts, was a rather abusive marriage. I could see it in her when her husband had been particularly hard on her. Even if there were no bruises or they were covered by the clothes. You could see it in her gaze and all her body language. Then I got such a desire to just hold her. I did that sometimes, too. In the room behind the back room, of course. I could see how she lit up. How she needed it. To be close with someone who wasn't harsh and gross to her but gentle and loving. Sometimes, it turned into us making love. I've rarely seen someone look so happy afterward. She really needed someone who loved her, even physically. It seemed like it loosened up a bit of her submissiveness if her husband had been too harsh to her the day before.

The Day I Was Caught off Guard

Nor was it there that I was caught red-handed. It was a completely different place where I hadn't expected it. And apparently, it was considered so serious that it was the reason why I was sent away from Lizzie-house.

It was autumn. Early autumn. First half of October. The place that Lizzie and her husband ran also included a small apple orchard. I had been sent there to pick the apples as they started to ripen. The apples would then be packed in plastic bags, and then they were sold in a small stall by the side of the road. The year before, there had been some thefts from that saucer, where people had to put some coins as payment. I had to sit at that stall for a couple of hours every afternoon. It was a rather boring job. But every now and then, someone would come by and buy a bag of apples. They were crispy and juicy.

One of those who often came was a young man who lived nearby. He was both handsome and seemed nice and sweet. We usually chatted a little together, and gradually, more and more. I quickly fell head over heels for him. I started playing Eve, who tempted Adam with an apple, and he was all for it.

After dinner, I snuck out again on the pretext that I would go for an extra run. Lizzie loved my runs. But the reason was that I was going to meet him. His name was Freddy. He waited at the agreed place, and then we walked a little way into a field road, a little bit into a cornfield where there were a few trees. Then we lay down in the grass there and made love. We loved each other, and we had nowhere else to go. We did this several times.

But the misfortune was that we had not gone far enough off the road. We could all too clearly be seen from the road. We hadn't thought of that. But some of the neighbors had come by on the road and had seen us lying there making love at full throttle and totally shameless, as they called it. And they had been outraged by this, so they had complained to Lizzie, whom I then had to face because of my shameless and immoral behavior, which completely went against the purpose of my social rehabilitation. And a lot of other nonsense of the same kind. She was very angry. But I think it was also because one of the people who had complained was the old angry head of the local authority's social services, who had threatened to take the care permit away from her so she would not be able to take people like me into care.

It was completely absurd. I was about to tell her about what was going on at the grocery store and about being a shirt girl for her husband, but she was busy and wouldn't listen to any excuses, she said, even before I got started.

The very next day, a rather tight-lipped, elderly lady from the social services of the municipality I came from, the one who had decided at the time that I should be placed with Lizzie, was there. She came up there by car and asked me to pack my things, and then I had to leave together with her right away. Because they couldn't accept my behavior, she said. The purpose was precisely to put me on an even keel so that I did not fall back into my old way of life of lying around with all sorts of random men. But when I could not manage to be in a place like this with freedom and responsibility, without squinting, so that it caused outrage among all the locals, then some other, more strict measures were needed. Now, I started to get nervous about where they were taking me. But she didn't want to say anything about that beforehand. She just said that they had found the right place for someone like me and that I should consider it a second chance they gave me. But that didn't make me any less nervous.

The Turn-around House

Now, I was taken to this new place that I didn't know anything about. I had my fears. But at least it wasn't a girls' home. They had said so. Nor was it a psychiatric ward. Perhaps some sort of light version of it, as I understood it. They had said that I should be 'hospitalized' and be a 'patient.' It didn't sound very good.

But it turned out that it wasn't that bad after all. There was no closed department. No straitjackets, no bars on the windows. I began to breathe a sigh of relief.

I had to talk to a psychiatrist once a week, and then I was given some pills. I also had to talk to a social worker. Her name was Susanna, and she was actually very nice. Significantly better than the caseworkers I had been exposed to up to that point.

I was going to be re-socialized, they said. To get me out of my loose way of life and into a more stable bourgeois life. In fact, I would like to do that myself. My old life had been a hard life in many ways. And I had been luckier than so many others. I hadn't become a drug addict like many did. The drugs were what had really ruined the life of many hookers. That was one of the reasons why I now had a serious desire to get out of the environment. I sincerely hoped that Connie had been as lucky as I was at that point. But I was concerned that I had not heard from her at all, and the letters I had sent to her came back with a stamp from the post office that said something like: *The addressee unknown by the address* because the post office had not been able to find her. Also, none of the people I had asked knew where she was, and I was afraid that was a bad sign. But there wasn't anything I could do about it.

In the beginning, I had enough to do with getting used to that new place. It was a bit special to be in such a place. Different from anything I had tried before. But it wasn't as bad as I had feared. It helped a little when I got to know a few of the others. One of them was Charlotte. She was a quiet girl. A different type than me. She had had a hard time with various things, including her parents having had a tough divorce after living as a dog and cat for many years. She was an only child and was in high school. She was very much the bookish type. She was sweet and sensible, but she lacked self-confidence and was easily knocked out if she had adversity.

She's attached herself to me a little bit. I think she saw me almost as a kind of big sister. She was somewhat younger than me. I tried to support her as best I could. During the day, I had to start on some activation projects. That's what they called it. Accordingly, it was only in the evening and night that I could be with her. In the evenings and the weekends, we often sat talking in a corner of the living room. She was curious to hear about my life, which was so different from hers.

On Sundays, we had fun, Charlotte and me. On Sundays, there was a large breakfast with oatmeal and cornflakes and milk and juice and soft-boiled eggs and freshly baked bread and cheese and jam of several kinds. I was not exactly used to that. Charlotte and I had developed our own little tradition around that Sunday breakfast. We showed up as some of the regulars every Sunday, and then we ate ourselves a hump of hot bread and soft-boiled eggs and everything else. It was almost like being in a hotel.

Afterward, we would both bring a cup of coffee and go out to the living room and hijack one of the Sunday newspapers, and then we would sit down in my room—each patient had a tiny single room—and then we sat there and read each of our sections of the Sunday newspaper and told each other if there was something interesting or something that was completely crazy or out of the question.

She was probably the one I talked to the most, and I enjoyed it, even though we were quite different in our backgrounds and such. And then there was Betty and Susan. I talked to them a lot, too. But otherwise, not so many young people were here. There weren't any guys worth collecting.

The place was called the turn-around house, and it was almost semi-official. On the official papers, it was called something else, but everyone called it so, including the employees. That's also what the place was called out and about in the city.

A couple of years ago, a new chief physician had been appointed leader of the place and he was not exactly what you would imagine a chief physician to be, and certainly not in such a place. He wasn't that old, probably only a couple of forty-something, and he put a lot of emphasis on being modern and progressive and stuff like that. He had developed such a little kind of philosophy about that name. He said that those who were there needed to turn around completely and get a new perspective on their lives. They were lying down; in some sense, they had been knocked down by something, and now they needed to hit a bump and turn around completely to get back on their feet. And that was what that place was supposed to help them with, he said.

At the Tin Can Factory

But I had to be re-socialized, so I had to start some job training, while at the same time, I had to be in the turn-around house in the evenings and nights and weekends. I was going to become a nice girl with a nice bourgeois life that any mother-in-law could be proud of. I had to get used to getting up in the morning and doing a regular salaried job. The social worker, Susan, had even gotten me a job. I was supposed to be an unskilled assistant at a small metal goods factory nearby. The kind of person who deals with various odd jobs of the kind that do not require any training or special qualifications, as it said in the piece of paper that she showed me about it.

It was something like cleaning up the warehouse, helping to pack items for shipping, brewing coffee, picking up beer, cleaning up the lunchroom when they had finished lunch, washing up their plates and coffee cups—by hand, with a dishwashing tub and rubber gloves—walking to the butcher on the corner and picking up sandwiches for their lunch every day. And keep the sandwich accounts precisely on dollars and cents. That is, only for some of them, as the other half of the workers brought a packed lunch. A very important thing was to sweep the floor in all the different rooms, which had to be done often and very thoroughly several times a day, and which resulted in me quickly getting the name 'Sweeper Girl,' and to the extent that they called me that instead of my name.

"Good morning, Sweeper Girl," they greeted me when I

arrived in the morning. The first few days, I corrected them and said that my name was Yvonne, but it completely bounced off them. And then it went on like this all day long.

"Come over here, Sweeper Girl."

"Have you put the coffee over, Sweeper Girl?"

"I think they need you out in the warehouse, Sweeper Girl."

"Can't you just pick up a bunch of lagers, Sweeper Girl?"

Or how about this one:

"Well, Sweeper Girl, are you enjoying the hot summer weather? But you don't have to wear trousers for us, Sweeper."

Of course, they weren't all bad, but many of them were. Apparently, that was just the tone of the place.

It was almost only men who were at the factory, and on Friday afternoon, they started drinking beer. It started shortly after lunch. There were about forty-five employees, and almost all of them were men.

Except for the two ladies in the bookkeeping, the switchboard lady, the director's secretary, and the sales manager's secretary, who were all mature women about fifty years or older. They did not participate in the Friday drinking but always stayed unapproachable in the offices on the second floor of a side building.

Friday drinking was only for those working at the factory itself, and as I said, it was only men. Most of them were middle-aged or at least over forty. And I had to participate too. I was also employed at the factory, they said. "You have to go to the party, Sweeper Girl," they told me. They wouldn't take no for an answer. I had to go there and be part of all the fun they had, as they put it. The first three Fridays, as it were.

There were a lot of things I had to get used to. I showed up at the factory at seven o'clock in the morning, so I didn't have time to have breakfast at the turn-around house before I left for work. One of the first things I had to do when I arrived was to start brewing coffee so that at least there was enough for the morning and for lunch. If there were some delayed coffee cups or anything else from the day before, then it should be washed up. I also had to go for a round and collect those who had been left around the workshops or elsewhere. Then, the floor had to be swept for the first time in the different rooms, and it should preferably be in a certain order. Then it was time to go to the butcher and pick up open sandwiches for those who had ordered them. And make sure you brought home the right ones because many of them had certain things they preferred and other things they didn't like. But it wasn't necessarily the same thing every week. I used a small cart when I had to pick up all the trays of open sandwiches. It had been provided with some extra shelves to put all the sandwiches on. Fortunately, it wasn't that far from the butcher shop, but you still had to be careful when you had to go over some crooked tiles or uneven cobblestones on the sidewalk.

Once I got back with the open sandwiches, I had to start setting the table for their lunch. Inside the lunchroom, so it was ready for lunch.

Setting the table for their lunch wasn't just plates and glasses and cutlery. But their beers, too. That was very important. The company provided a beer for their lunch. They could choose which one it should be if it wasn't too special. But back then, there weren't many different kinds of beer. They got the same kind of beer every day.

There were fixed seats in the lunchroom, and I had to hurry to learn the seating of them all, so I knew them by heart. And then, I also had to learn to remember who was drinking what kind of beer so I could put the right beer next to each seat. They would be mad if I had swapped them and given any of them the wrong kind of beer.

One of the first days, they did a trick on me with those beers. It was on the Friday of the first week. I had really made an effort to learn by heart who sat where, what they were called, and if they had a nickname. And the most important thing, what kind of beer they preferred. I had checked it and double-checked it, and then just checked it one more time to be sure I had done it right. Of course, I had first written it all down on a piece of paper to make sure I didn't remember anything wrong.

They told me to drink the beers I had put wrong. I took it easy because I had been so careful about it. But they had swapped some of the beers around while I was in a back room doing something else. And now they claimed that I was the one who had put them wrong. And that I should now drink all the sixteen beers that they said I had put wrong. And they all had to be gulped down during lunch break and early afternoon, so I would be drunk all day.

I would not normally have had so much against it. I have seldom refused to get so many beers at someone else's expense. The problem was that I had to do that now. Because I was at the Turnaround house, they ran a total zero tolerance for alcohol. It was probably because quite a few of those who were there had a history of heavy drinking, and if I came home to the place and was drunk, it would be fatal. At the turn-around house, they kept a strict course where no excuses were accepted. It was zero alcohol—with no excuses or you were stuck out. It was unconditional grounds for expulsion from the site. And then you didn't always know where you ended up instead.

I had to stand firm and refuse those sixteen free beers they wanted to pour into me. By now, I had decided to stay at the turn-around house and go through their re-soc program. After a month there, I had already bought the idea of being re-socialized, and this was not least the merit of social worker Susan. I didn't want to risk being kicked out because I came home drunk. And no matter what I thought of the turn-around house, it certainly was not those idiots at the tin factory who had to decide whether I should be there or not. I said NO, one more time and insisted.

One of them later explained to me that it was an old tradition that with a new apprentice, they did that trick on him. So that from the start, he could get to know his place at the bottom of the pecking order. And accordingly let all his guards down and completely expose himself when he was drunk. Then you knew where they had him.

But there was no apprentice in the company now, so I was the one who ended up in that role. By the way, I guess I also did a lot of the things that they used to put a first-year apprentice to.

But in order not to lose face, they apparently thought that they would have to find something else violent and offensive for me to do when I now categorically maintained my refusal of the sixteen beers. So they came up with something really gross and disgusting. And if I also refused to do what they had planned for me now, they would tell the staff at the turn-around house that I had turned up an hour late this morning and had been so drunk that I had been sleeping it out in the warehouse most of the day. But that was not true! That was a blatant lie, I objected.

Well, that would be my word against theirs, they said. And who did I think they would believe the most at the turn-around house? The foreman at the factory or me?

I knew that. They would believe what my superior, the foreman, said. He was my boss. And he was one of those who led this. The fact that a new employee had to be put in place at the bottom of the hierarchy immediately was probably just part of his management style.

It was no use protesting. What they had come up with, should not be that hard for someone with my background, one of them said.

"Well, what did he mean by that?" I asked. "Well, you'll see in a minute," he said.

The idea they had come up with was completely far-fetched. But I had to do it. Now, I had become stubborn. Not want to be thrown out of the Turnaround House because of such idiotic nonsense. It had become a matter of principle for me. Apparently, those at the factory had decided that I had to be humiliated in some way to continue in my re-soc job at the tin factory. I had to try to take it with my head held high. I didn't want to give it up. When I encounter this kind of resistance, it just makes me more stubborn and more determined that I g o o n w i t h what I have started—even if I have otherwise been a little lukewarm about it.

Then, I had to put up with the humiliation they had planned for me, even though it was completely unreasonable. I didn't even know what it was. It shouldn't be until they'd had lunch, they said.

What they had come up with, was that they would all stay in the lunchroom, they all stayed in the lunchroom. That is, five of them sat on separate chairs at one end of the room, up against the wall where the large bulletin board was. Everyone else would sit and watch as spectators. Then I had to stand up facing all the spectators and pull off my blouse and bra, so I had bare breasts, and show them off a little. Then I had to go to the first of the men in front of the bulletin board, number one in the row. He sat with his legs together. I had to sit on his knees facing him. Then I had to unbuckle the belt of his trousers and put my hand down behind his waistband and grab his penis and run it off with my hand until it went on him. Meanwhile, I also had to put up with him fondling my breasts. And then on to the next in line until I'd been through all five of them.

Meanwhile, one of the others took time out with a stopwatch to see how long it had taken to release each of them. And the one who had come the fastest was then declared the winner, and there was a second and a number three as if it was a perverted Olympic sports performance. It was then written on a large piece of paper that was put up on the bulletin board. Another of the spectators had taken a lot of pictures of it, and a few days later, a new note appeared on the bulletin board, with a picture of me and a picture of him who had become number one, and a red heart drawn around it, and underneath it said: 'Girlfriend potential?'

It was completely absurd. Especially when you consider that my work at the tin factory was part of a rehabilitation project that was to transform me from one of the street's easy-going girls into a nice and respectable daughter-in-law candidate, it was almost a joke.

I feel sorry for the apprentices if that was also the kind of thing they were exposed to. Perhaps under the threat of losing the apprenticeship if they do not comply.

I've heard some people saying afterward, "Well, it's probably because she's a whore that she agreed to do that so willingly."

No, it wasn't. On the contrary, it was because I had now become so determined on that re-soc project that I wouldn't let those idiots ruin it, so I was kicked out of it because of such nonsense. And, of course, it was humiliating and unpleasant.

That is completely unreasonable, regardless of the background you come up with. But my background, where I had tried a little of everything, probably helped me get through it more easily than if I had been very young and innocent. Then I don't know what I should have done. Then, I would probably have gone out of the turn-around house and out of my re-soc program because I had lacked the courage to put up with that humiliation instead of getting drunk.

But there are some people who think that if you have once been into prostitution like I have, you just stand up for anything because you have no boundaries or reservations about anything of the sort. Yes, of course you have. Of course, you have the right to say no to something you don't like, just like everyone else.

It just had to be said.

Whew, it was a worse game. The men considered it a great introduction to a terrific version of the weekly Friday drinking, which started after lunch and lasted the rest of the afternoon, right up until the end of the day when many of them went out into the city and continued. I would probably have done that myself earlier. But now I was sitting there, the only girl with about thirty-five men, and had to make do with a Coca-Cola for the sake of the turn-around house and their strict course against alcohol. And it's not much fun to be the only girl among so many half-drunk men who were only too aware of my past. It was only the workers at the factory who participated in that Friday drinking, 'the ones on the floor.' The very few white-collar employees and the office ladies and the bosses stayed away. Except for the foreman, who almost acted like he was in charge of all this.

The first three Fridays, as I said, I had to be part of it. It was simply expected of me. The very next Friday, the second week I was there, I once again got a minor shock when I saw what they had used to decorate the large bulletin board in the lunchroom. They had gathered about ten of the pin-up girls from some newspaper, and then they had pasted my face onto all of them. They were some of the pictures from the week before that the photographer guy had magnified and cut my face out of. I was furious. What the hell were they thinking? But then the foreman came over and asked if I didn't have a sense of humor. It was just good-natured workshop humor, he said, and I had better get used to it if I didn't want to make it too difficult for myself.

But then, in the fourth week, something happened. Something completely different. What happened was that the director had a cousin – or second cousin, I think – named Carl. He was a rather special type. He was in his late sixties and had probably tried his hand at many things without really succeeding at anything. He was not an employee of the company. Probably, he had been in the past. Now, he was retired. But every Friday, he delivered goods for them. Only one day a week. And only small batches of goods for some of the smaller customers out and about. It was a job he had been given because the director wanted to help a disadvantaged family member. But now Carl had asked for me to go with him. To help him unload the goods, he had said. After all, he was by now an elderly man approaching seventy. The director had agreed to that. In the fourth week, I was at the company; that's what I was going to do on Fridays.

Driving Carl's Car

I was a bit excited about it the first Friday in the new way. As usual, I showed up at seven o'clock in the morning, and then I had to brew coffee as usual, so there was enough for the morning and lunch. At eight o'clock, Carl arrived in his old van. And it was very old. I had never seen a car like that before. It was very special.

We started out by loading goods into the car. It didn't take long because it was only some minor deliveries to some small customers. The company's two trucks took care of the larger deliveries.

When we were about to get in the car, it turned out that I was the one who was going to drive. Carl had lost his driver's license after he had been caught several times for drunk driving, he explained to me with a downturned look after I had loudly wondered why I suddenly had to be the driver because that was not the explanation I had been given.

Well, that's how it was, he said, sounding completely ashamed. But they were not allowed to know that at the factory, nor the director, because then he risked losing the job of delivering goods. And he wanted to continue to do so. So that's why he wanted me to come along. I had to promise him loud and holy that I wouldn't tell anyone.

It was not one of the company's cars. It was Carl's own old bucket of a van. Not only was it old and scratchy, but it was also very special. He said it was from 1952, so it was about twenty years old. It was a type of car I had never seen before. It only had three wheels. There was only a single front wheel. But even though it was a three-wheeler, it wasn't a mini car. It was the size of a Volkswagen box wagon, maybe a bit longer. The small engine sat on top of the single front wheel, so the entire engine turned around with the front wheel when you turned the steering wheel. The engine pulled the front wheel with chain drive, just like on a motorcycle.

But Carl sounded like he was completely carried away by talking about it. He'd had it from new, he said. Then he set about explaining how to drive it. How the gears lay, and all that kind of stuff. The gear lever sat on the dashboard, like some weird kind of umbrella handle. It had freewheeling like most two-strokes, and you had to get used to that, he said. The steering might feel a little heavy because there was so much weight on the front wheel, and it felt a little different because there was only one front wheel. And you had to keep an extra good distance from cyclists and parked cars because the cargo box was wider than the cab, and the rear wheels were even on the outside of the goods box, so it took up more space at the rear than you expected.

It started willingly enough when I turned the ignition key, but it made an awful noise. However, it helped a bit when I switched up in the second and third gear with that lever on the dashboard.

We were going down south. I drove slowly and carefully. I had to get used to that strange vehicle that I had suddenly become the driver of. None of us said much. But I couldn't help but laugh when I asked what kind of car brand it was, because I hadn't seen one like that before. He said the car brand was called 'TEMPO.' It had to be a joke because it was certainly not a fast runner. But the word TEMPO even stood in large letters across the bonnet.

After nearly an hour, Carl told me to stop by a hotel where there was a restaurant on the ground floor. Well, what was that all about, I thought. First the restaurant, then a hotel room, or what? But I parked the car and obediently followed Carl into the hotel restaurant. It seemed like he knew the place and was a well-known guest there.

We went into the restaurant. Carl had even booked a table in advance. He would pay for the lunch, he said. It seemed that he wasn't in a hurry because we sat there for almost one hour while we had lunch, and I wondered what he was up to. As he got four or five beers on board, he became very talkative, and by the time we got to the coffee, he was already telling me his life story. I waited for what he had up his sleeve next. But nothing happened except that he finally got hold of a waiter and paid. And then out to the car and continue the trip, which now went west. Following Carl's instructions, we stuck to the slightly smaller roads.

When we reached the city in question, we just had to find the small coffee and tea shop where the tin cans should be delivered. But Carl knew the way well and had probably been there many times before. It was some coffee cans with the store's logo that they should have delivered. He eagerly talked about all these kinds of things.

After I carried the cans into the store's small warehouse, Carl and I were invited to the coffee shop by the owner and his wife for afternoon coffee. Then Carl and the two of them sat chatting together like old friends for over half an hour while I was getting more and more bored.

Finally, their coffee session was over, and we could move on. Carl had at least three glasses of cognac with his coffee, and he had to lean on me when we walked back to the car.

Then there were just two more small deliveries. Fortunately, both places were too busy to invite us in.

Then we had a long drive back to the factory. Now Carl had fallen asleep and was snoring, so I had to find my own way, and I succeeded, even though I did make a few small detours at first. It was a boring trip. There was no radio in the old van, so the only sounds were the noise of the engine and Carl's loud snoring.

But we made it back to the factory. I parked the car. I also had to get used to parking it because it was also a little different than I was used to. Partly because of the single front wheel and partly because it was quite a large wagon to maneuver around in a parking lot where the cars were close.

Carl was still asleep. I tried to wake him up. No luck. Well, he just had to sit there and sleep it off. But now the foreman came out of the factory and over to the car that I was about to get out of. He said that I couldn't just let Carl sit there and sleep. "I had to drive him home and get him into bed," he said.

WHAT? Had it now become my job to have the old drunkard brought home and put to bed? I protested and said my workday was over. In fact, it was also half an hour past work time. But no, it wasn't because that was something he decided. There was such a thing as ordered overtime, he reminded me. And this was a job he imposed on me as my boss. There was no way around it. He gave me the address and explained which way to go. It wasn't that far away, he said. Only about ten minutes.

Full of inner protest, I got back into the car and fished the car keys out of Carl's pocket where I had put them. He was still sleeping heavily and snoring as before. Fortunately, it was not that difficult to find the settlement where he lived. I parked the car and then proceeded to wake him up. I even coaxed the keys to the apartment out of his pocket. Fortunately, he lived on the ground floor. I had him piloted through the door and into the bedroom, so it was the bed he went down on and not the floor. I put the car keys on the coffee table in the living room, along with the street door key, as the foreman had told me to. Then, out the door again, slamming it behind me, and then I had to go back to the factory so I could pick up my bike and hurry back to the turn-around house before they finished dinner. But I was lucky; I just managed to get into the dining room before they were about to clean off, so I managed to get myself a portion of dinner before it was all carried out.

It was a bit of a rough start to my new Fridays.

That was pretty much the pattern for the coming Fridays, too. However, it wasn't every time I had to drive Carl home and put him to bed. It varied a bit where we had to deliver the tin cans, but it was mostly down south. Apparently, it was Carl's district for that kind of delivery. The long lunch at the hotel became a regular feature, and each time, he told me a new part of his life story. He also usually fell asleep on the return trip. But he was nice enough when you had just gotten used to him. He didn't try anything.

Once, after a few months, we were going to another town with some goods. This time, it was down the coast. We even had lunch somewhere else than we used to. We didn't sit as long over lunch as we used to. After lunch, we continued to a small town where some cans of some kind were also to be delivered.

But hey, wasn't that where Connie's aunt lived? The one who had forced Connie's baby to be given up for adoption. Could it be if this was the place where Connie was—far away from everything—and that's why I hadn't been able to find her in any of the usual places? And that none of the people I asked knew where she was.

But I had no idea where in this town her aunt lived. I didn't know her name either. It would be a difficult task to find her. And I didn't even know if that was where Connie was.

For the time being, we had to go and deliver those tin cans to some small shop. Then followed once again a long-winded afternoon coffee. It was incredible so many of the places where it was Carl's acquaintances and old friends who invited us in for coffee. I strongly suspected that it was mostly for the fun of it that Carl drove out with those small deliveries of different tin items. It couldn't possibly be profitable. But that wasn't my problem. That day, I just sat there and was even more bored than usual.

Finally, they were finished. Then, there were just two more places where we had to go in and drop something off. However, it was only one of them where we were offered coffee and cake – and a couple of cognacs for Carl.

On the way back, I drove around some residential streets, hoping that something would turn up. And suddenly, my eyes widened. Out of an older villa, someone came out the garden path toward a white Chevrolet parked at the curb. Someone I just had to take a closer look at. It was a middle-aged woman, a man of similar age, and a young girl. The girl looked a lot like Connie! But I only saw her from behind when I was driving because she walked halfway toward the other two, who rushed at her as if they were busy and needed to do something. Before I had gotten there and stopped the car, they had already gotten into the Chevy that started and drove away.

I let go of the brake and stepped on the accelerator instead. There was only one thing to do. I just had to follow them and see where they were going—and if it was really Connie. I couldn't miss that chance. The only thing to do was to follow the Chevy. Even if Carl complained all that he wanted. Strangely enough, he hadn't fallen asleep yet, as he often used to do on the return trip. It would otherwise have been very convenient.

It was a longer trip than I had expected. A whole little car chase. But it was probably mostly me who perceived it as a car chase because it was difficult for me to keep up with the other car. The white Chevy drove fast as if they had an appointment and were late. Or maybe they had noticed that there was a weird old car that kept following them, so they tried to get away from me. But they should not be allowed to do so. I did what I could to not be left behind.

It was more difficult on the straight stretches because there the Chevy could speed up, and the old Tempo van could be pushed up to seventy km per hour at most, and then it should even go downhill. At least when there was a load on, but there wasn't now, so it helped a bit.

The old three-wheeler was better at getting around the corners once I had gotten some practice in it, and I actually started to enjoy driving it around the corners a little hard while Carl sat and looked completely startled.

However, I managed to hang on. But it was a somewhat longer drive than I had expected. We had come out of town and a few miles away to a small neighboring town. Finally, the white Chevy stopped in front of a slightly older villa in a large garden. I jumped out of the car as soon as I had it stopped, but by accident, I pressed the switch to the horn so that it stuck. All three of the people entering the garden gate turned around and stared, both the man and the woman and the young girl they had with them.

It was Connie!

Now, I was sure it was her.

"Connie!" I shouted as loudly as I could, and almost at the

same time, she yelled, "Yvonne!" And then I just ran to where she stood, and we gave each other a huge hug.

But the two she was with, one of whom was probably the aunt, were already rushing at her. "Connie, what are you doing? Come on!" she shouted.

So, very reluctantly, we had to detach ourselves from each other before we had finished hugging.

"Connie," I shouted, "give me your address and phone number." She yelled the phone number at me as they practically dragged her along. I kept repeating it to myself so as not to forget it.

I went back to the car that was standing there with the engine running. As soon as I got in, I asked, "Carl, do you have anything to write with?" Fortunately, he had a pen and even some paper, so I could have it written down right away while I remembered it and still knew the phone number by heart. I also wrote down the house number, drove to the end of the road where the street name was, and wrote it down as well. Admittedly, I didn't know if this was where she lived or if they had come there to visit somebody.

But now we turned around and drove back to the town we came from. Because we had to go back and deliver some goods. I followed Carl's instructions, and soon I was waiting impatiently again for another coffee get-together at another of Carl's old friends.

When we stopped at a red light on our way out of town, an old Volkswagen with three young guys pulled up next to us. They laughed loudly and pointed their fingers at Carl's old three-wheeler and asked if we should race to the next traffic light. Of course, it was just to humiliate me. Normally, I wouldn't have reacted to something like that at all. But now I suddenly wanted to, so I gave signs back that I took up the challenge. They laughed even louder at that. But I had noticed that even though the old antiquity of a car had a rather low top speed, it was more versatile than you would think. That is, if you pushed it a little.

When the traffic lights went from red to green, I stepped on the accelerator. Quickly change gears, step on it, change gears again, step on it. I gave it everything it could pull while Carl had woken up from his half-slumber and was now clinging to the handle in the door, asking, startled, "What are you doing with my car?"

"I'm just defending its honor," I replied, without taking my eyes off the road and the Volkswagen lying in the lane on the left.

And then we succeeded! I reached the next red light about twenty seconds before the boys in the Volkswagen. You should have seen the expression on their faces. It was a sight for gods. Oh my god, how I rejoiced!

Then Carl had to scold me a little about my driving. Normally, I don't do anything like racing any more. It was only because I was in a special mood that day and because those guys provoked me.

On the rest of the return trip, nothing special happened.

Picking up Connie

During the following weeks, things continued as usual. I was still in the turn-around house; I still worked four days a week as a service girl at the tin can factory. They had started calling me that. It was the foreman who had come up with it because I had complained that they called me 'Sweeper Girl' instead of using my name. After I said that, he looked a little pensive for a moment. Then he said, "Yes, I understand you. And maybe you're right. It's misleading. Because you're doing a lot more than just sweeping the floor, we should probably focus a little more on that. So, in the future, I think we'll call you Service Girl. After all, it fits much better. Then people can put in it whatever they want."

And with that, the discussion was closed. From then on, I was called Service Girl by everyone in the factory. All the men, at least. And I had almost nothing to do with the office ladies.

So now, for example, "Come here, Service Girl." Or:

"I think Jimmy needs you, Service Girl." Or,

"Will you do me a big favor, Service Girl?" And so on.

That were the first four days of the week. On Fridays, I continued to drive for Carl, and I was happy to get away from the rough tone of the foreman and the others at the factory. That is to Carl's credit. He always behaved like a gentleman when it came to that sort of thing. He never touched me. He never tried anything. Nor were there any remarks about my background. There was only one time when he alluded a little to my old profession, and it was quite innocent. He had recently got a girlfriend of roughly the same age after probably living alone for a few years. And now he asked me a little shyly if I could give him a few tips on how to satisfy her a little better than he apparently did, which she was a little unhappy with. And I knew a lot about that, so I gave him a few tips about it, and a few Fridays later, he said that he had tried my advice and the small tricks I had told him—and they worked, so now she was much happier with him, and they had even talked about getting married next spring. It was so sweet and innocent.

But unfortunately, there were no more trips to the town where I had spotted Connie.

But now I had gotten Connie's phone number so I could call her. I thought so. But it wasn't that easy. Back then, there was no question of each person having their own cell phone. When Connie lived with her aunt and her aunt's husband, there was only one phone in the house. A landline-phone. If you called up to talk to Connie, for example, it was very often one of the others who picked up the phone and then explained if she was home and if she had time to talk on the phone.

But that was not the case here. Every time I called, it was either the aunt or her husband who picked up the phone and said in a very dismissive voice that Connie was busy and didn't have time to talk on the phone, and then the phone was hung up. I tried many times, but each time, the result was the same.

I had written down the address of where they took her that day with the white Chevy, but I wasn't sure if that was where she lived. It turned out that, in fact, it was not. I later found out that it was just a place where the aunt knew someone and where they drove Connie twice a week because she apparently had to help them in the house with something for a couple of hours before they came and picked her up again late at night. But that's a whole other story.

But on the other hand, I found her real address, where she lived with her aunt and her aunt's husband or boyfriend, or whatever it was. And it was very simple. I had the phone number, and then I called the Directory Information and was told who had that phone number. Complete with name and address. So now I started writing letters to Connie. But I didn't get anything out of it either. They didn't even come back. She just never answered any of them. She later said she had never gotten any of them. It must have been the aunt or her husband who had snatched them as soon as they came through the letterbox to cut her off from contact with someone from her old environment.

They probably knew perfectly well who I was.

So now, I had to come up with something if I wanted to get in touch with Connie again. It wasn't long before I got an idea for a way to do it when the easy solutions didn't work.

I no longer saw much of my parents. They didn't like my profession and what they called my social decline. I came from a nice bourgeois home, and they were disappointed in me – that I hadn't graduated, nor gotten married or engaged, now that I was twenty-five years old. And above all, my amoral existence, as they called it, was like a street chick who threw herself in the shoes of anyone and sold herself to random men for money. But they hadn't broken my hand either, nor had I broken with them, but the relationship between us had become a little strained, and we didn't see each other very often. There had also been a few loud arguments in between. I'm an only child, so I didn't have any siblings to support me.

But I still had a key to their townhouse from ancient times, even though it had been a very long time since I had used it. And now I have got a postcard from them. They were on holiday in the Caribbean. It had been their preferred form of vacation for some years. They had just arrived and were supposed to be there for two weeks, they wrote. Now, I started getting ideas. The next Saturday, I got off from the turn-around house because I had to go home to my parents—I said.

You could easily get time off for that at the weekend. They even considered it a step forward that I was now apparently resuming contact with my parents.

And there it was. The old blue Oldsmobile that they had had ever since I was a child. It was a four-door with two-tone paintwork in light blue and dark blue. I unlocked the door, and it started right away. It was a bit nostalgic. I backed out of the garage, locked the garage door, and then I drove off. Down to find Connie. But I could see that the fuel gauge was very low. It seemed like the tank was almost empty, so I had to refuel somewhere before too long. I hadn't thought of that at all. Of course, I didn't have a lot of cash on me. As an inpatient at the Turn-around house, I only got a small amount of pocket money each month. When I was still working as a street hooker, I had been used to having a lot more money in my hands. Now, I only had a few dollars on me. And back then, I had no credit cards. Now, what to do? It was idiotic that I hadn't thought that far.

But this was not to be allowed to get in my way. After all, I had the background I had, and at the gas station, there were at least three truck drivers and a few others who looked like they needed to relieve the pressure. Need I say more? I filled the tank completely and even got a whole small bundle of dollar bills to stick in my pocket. Of course, it had delayed me somewhat, but I didn't have a fixed schedule to keep.

When I started the car again and was about to drive out of

the tank, I suddenly changed my mind. I parked the car and went in and bought a Coke, a bag of candy, and a bun of some sort to eat. I just had to sit down for ten minutes or more and digest the contrasts or contradictory things or whatever the heck it was that popped up into my head and put them in place before I drove on.

I finally reached the town. I had to ask for directions a few times before I found the place. The next problem was getting hold of Connie. Was she even home? And I couldn't just ring the doorbell. It was probably the aunt or her husband who would open the door, and they wouldn't let me talk to Connie. My plan suddenly didn't seem very well thought out.

Now what? It was now about half past eight in the evening. It had taken longer than I expected to find the place. I went to the house and rang the doorbell. That's where they drove her once a week. They also used to come and pick her up again later in the evening. I tried to explain that they had not been able to get there themselves and had sent me to pick her up instead. It went easy enough. Then we drove back home, I mean to the big city, where Connie was initially installed in my little pink apartment, and then I had to go to my parent's house to put the car back in the garage. I made sure to put it exactly as it was before and put the car keys where I had taken them. I didn't have the courage to tell them the whole story of why I had borrowed the car. It was best they didn't notice. Otherwise, I would be showered with all sorts of questions when they got home. I made sure that everything was exactly as before, and no one could see that there had been anyone. Then maybe I could explain it all later. But afterward, I remembered that my father would probably wonder about one thing. I had refueled it, so the tank was completely full, and when I put the car in the garage, the gas meter still showed that the tank was just over half full. When I started out, it had been almost empty. My father was just the type of person who would notice this kind of thing and wonder about it when they got home.

And then we went by the bus to the pink apartment. We had a lot to tell each other, and during the night, we wrote a nice letter to Connie's aunt about how Connie was in good hands in a super place of resocialization, where she had been given a great chance, so they shouldn't be worried about her. Both the name and address of the place were, of course, made up but were worded so vaguely and so close to sounding like a place that existed, so we figured it would work.

Connie Is Back

It also went well for a while, and everything was back to normal—for better or worse. Because it wasn't all happy days, it was often both hard and violent, and I don't really understand why we went back to it ourselves. Of course, there was pressure on us that should not be underestimated. There were many rough types among the men who did what they could to keep us in it—simply because they used us as a kind of money-making machine. We had also become accustomed to having a much larger consumption and much more money in our hands than we could have had with a regular job. Fortunately, none of us have gotten on drugs. I know there were many other prostitutes who had a much harder life than us. And I do hope that no one sees this as an advertisement for prostitution or as an attempt to downplay all the many dark sides there are to it. But that's how I experienced it when I think back. At the time, I might have described some of it in a more violent way.

Some may also wonder why I write so much about things other than what is directly about being a prostitute. But that's because there were a lot of other things in my life, too. And because it quickly becomes a lot of trivial repetition if it's only about being a prostitute and the tons of strange men you're exposed to. But this is not a book written to depict being a prostitute. There are probably many others who can do that much better. This is, first and foremost, a book about Connie and me and our lives and experiences together and when we were alone.

Just so it doesn't get misunderstood. I can tell you that, yes, it seemed to be fine at first, after Connie was back among those she knew, and I was also there almost daily because that's where it was happening. But I had my pink place I could retreat to if it got too hard for me. And yet, it was not quite the same as it had been. The environment was starting to get tougher, and it didn't take very long before Connie's aunt found out about our scam and found out that she was back there; she turned up accompanied by someone from the social services and brought her back to this small town where she lived.

Me at a Household School

Shortly after, I left the whole environment. Now, I had been sent away again. Far away from the red-light district and to a small town in the countryside.

I was sent to a household school where there were only women. Thirty-five young women who had to learn housekeeping so they could become good housewives. I think that was the idea. Most of them were younger than me. They were nice to me. The teachers at the school were also women. It was an all-female universe. I don't know if that was part of the idea behind it as well. It started right after the summer holidays and was supposed to last a year. A whole school year. Daily life took its course without major fluctuations. It was pretty much all right, except I was quite bored.

As I mentioned, Connie had been sent away to that aunt of hers again. After all, she rode her almost like a mare. A daily nightmare almost. She had been to pick her up again, her aunt. She was a friend of those social workers and the whole system, apparently. Connie had been sent away again. As well as me being deported to some random household school far away. If that could make them happy.

About nine months passed like that. I was almost starting to get used to the daily grind there on the spot. We lived there, too. It was a boarding school. I basically only socialized with the other girls at the school.

Then one day a letter came to me. It was from Connie! She

had returned to the big city again. Some dubious types from her aunt's town had taken her back there and had been touring with her for a week. Put more bluntly, they exploited her well and truly. And then she had seen her chance to come back to the red-light district. She might have almost gotten some sort of fixation on that spot. Or maybe it was even worse to be with her aunt. Later, she told me a great deal about the mail order company where she had been put in charge of working in the warehouse and packing parcels in a way that could have been done by a robot all day long, at an absolutely underpaid salary, and where the young and half-old men, quickly found out too much about her past and found a dark corner of the warehouse, where, in turn, they could exploit her as roughly as they wanted without her daring to resist. And apparently, without the oh-so-nice and morally high-strung aunt knowing anything about what was going on. They threatened her to shut up and say nothing to her aunt. After some months, she suddenly got a chance to get away, as three of the men from the warehouse wanted to celebrate the birthday of one of them by taking her to the big city and the red-light district, getting her drunk, and touring her for a week. It was her ticket to going back to what must have been like a paradise in comparison. But, of course, I was not told all that until later.

She must have gotten my address at the household school from Marianne or Ulla, a couple of the other hookers. Super nice. I read her letter again and again.

Running Away to Meet Connie

The very next day, I had made my decision. When Connie could go on a jumping trip—or whatever you wanted to call it, so could I. After dinner, I came up with a pretext to go for a little walk. I came out of the school, hurried away, and to a rest area where the truck drivers often stopped to have a meal. I had no money either for a train ticket or anything, so I had to make the trip as a hitchhiker.

It was quite quickly possible for me to hitchhike a truck that was going to the big city with a load of something. I knew that I would have to pay for the trip with my body, but I didn't care.

He got what he wanted, and I don't even bother going into detail about it. It delayed us a bit. He even promised to drive me all the way to the red-light district. Then I had to find Connie. I was around a few places before I found her with Maria, and I was allowed to stay there for the first nights. But first, we hugged really well and thoroughly, and we had a lot to tell each other, so there wasn't much sleep the first night.

The Art of Eating Money Bills

This is based on an old text I wrote back then. For some reason, I wrote in the third person about myself.

She had had some bad years. She had been down in the dirt. But after all, she had been more fortunate than Connie. They had been close friends back then, sticking together through thick and thin. But then they had become separated. Was it she who had disappeared? Or was it Connie who had disappeared? Which of them had disappeared the most? Stupid question, but it had plagued her for several years at the time. Maybe she was the one who had failed? And had left Connie behind? How had she managed since then? She had searched for her in so many places, first the old places from that time. But in vain. Where had she gone? It was such a long time since she had last held her and hugged her. She missed her so much.

She remembered one special evening some years ago. A totally wild and far-out evening. Connie is at her worst. It must have been one of the last times she was with her. Then, she had been far away for several years.

They had, of course, gone to the tavern. It was kind of a night off for all of them. It had been a pretty good day as far as customers were concerned. Mostly tourists. We could almost pick and choose between them. Which of them would we take first? Or whoever we'd rather not have at all. At least, that's how I remember it. Most of them paid well. It had been a really good day.

And it was in summer. Early summer. There was a real summer atmosphere. Such a cool atmosphere that it was party time now. And Connie was among those leading the way. She was absolutely thrilled. After all, it wasn't that she had decided that she didn't want to take more customers that day. That's not how it worked. And certainly not for Connie. Now, it was just a party, and you could always change your mind along the way if you were suddenly short of money, for example. Connie was not into fixed principles. Principles were there to be broken. But that's how we all felt. Living in the moment and letting random inspiration and your whims lead you. It was more like that.

We were probably all a little intoxicated by that summer atmosphere. It was early June, I think, one of the first real hot summer days. We had earned a lot of money, and we had all had something to drink during the day. Not least, Connie. I hadn't held back, but Connie had really gone for it. By late afternoon, she had been too drunk to have any more customers. She was starting to get rough in her mouth when she got too much to drink. It scared customers away and gave the place a bad name. Those nice, wealthy tourists could be very sensitive to that kind of thing.

But in the evening, we had gone to one of the taverns. Now it was party time. With Connie in the lead. As I said, she was in high spirits. But it was the kind of high spirits that could turn around and suddenly go the opposite way into something completely crazy. You never quite knew about Connie when she was in that mood.

Money does not smell, they say. But they taste like hell, she said. She repeated this often. And she had to know. She had tried it herself.

It was René who made her do it. The one with that dollar bill. That night. And Kenny. At least he agreed. They bet they couldn't get her to eat a $100 bill. Yes, she was going to literally bite it and chew it and swallow it and everything. Bit by bit, the whole dollar bill. Otherwise, it did not apply. They had bet on it. It was nonsense, and she only did it because she was drunk already.

Kenny and René claimed that she couldn't. That she could not eat it or that she simply couldn't bring herself to do it when it came down to it. They didn't believe she could.

But then Connie became stubborn. She wouldn't have it said about her that she was such a jerk. So now she had to show them that she could. But she took the time to do so. Now, they all did. First, the whole gang had to look at the banknote, which Kenny fumbled out of his trouser pocket because René did not have that kind of money on him at all. At least, he claimed so. But that note had to go all the way around, from hand to hand, so that everyone around the table could approve it and check that it was okay. That there was no fiddling with it. It took time because everyone just thought they should do it really thoroughly. And preferably, just make a few quick remarks about that, too. There were also a few who were stupid enough to just try to see if they could get away with stealing it and even stuffing it in their pocket and then pretending it had gone to the floor or claiming that it was another one who had stolen it. But it was immediately discovered, and the three in question were sentenced one by one to buy beers for everyone as a punishment.

But in the end, that old dollar bill had been all around and had been approved everywhere, even if it took time. But then Brian suddenly interfered. He took it from the one who had the dollar bill in his hand and stuck it into a glass of whiskey. A glass of whiskey on the rocks. Like that's what he was drinking at the time. He rolled up the dollar bill and dipped it into his whiskey a few times. It was completely soaked in whiskey when he pulled it up and gave it to Connie, whom he was probably quite fond of. I think he did it to help her. So that it tasted better.

But it was immediately declared cheating and fraud by René, Kenny, and several others. Then it would be too easy for her, they said. Then it was wet and soaked and tasted like whiskey, and then it would be too easy for her to eat it. It was cheating compared to what they had bet on. They argued for a while. Brian was about to get into a fight with Kenny about it.

There were a couple of tourists sitting in the corner, and they came over and wanted to hear what it was all about.

Then the tourists asked what was being celebrated. Brian said that Connie and himself were going to get married in a few weeks. But it was just a lie and wishful thinking because Connie didn't want someone like Brian at all. He loved her, he said, but she didn't even bother to look in his direction. He certainly wasn't the father. Although Connie was pregnant, it turned out later. No one knew anything about that yet, not even herself. Then she would have told me and a few other girls. It was after that very hot affair she'd had with that office guy Jansen was his name, whom she suddenly went back to and became his lover again after he had otherwise been thrown out six months before. But it only lasted a month, that new affair with Jansen.

But those tourists wanted to take some pictures of the young married couple expecting a child together. We didn't think Connie would agree to that. But now she reacted quickly and said that yes, they could do that, but it would cost them 150 bucks as a wedding gift. They agreed to that, and Connie was hugging Brian for the first and only time ever, and those tourists took a lot of pictures of them.

Then, the whole thing about eating that money bill was resumed. Connie slowly and solemnly tore a small corner of the banknote and put the small piece of paper in her mouth, all eyes on her. The tourists, although they sat a little further away, looked amazed. Then she began to chew. We could see that it was not easy for her. But then she took a sip of beer and had it washed down.

She was about to continue with the next little bite, but then things started to get going. A drunken sailor had entered the tavern. He had been there before and often been a customer of Connie's. Connie sat down at the table again, took a sip of beer, and then she was ready to continue the bet. Of course, she was also strongly encouraged to do so, so she didn't just drop it. She continued quietly. One more bite, and one more, and one more, and another. She chewed and chewed and swallowed and swallowed. It took time, but it seemed to be going perfectly well. She had gotten into a good rhythm with it, it seemed.

But then came a new disturbance. Two men had entered the tavern, and they asked for 'the one with the beautiful tattoos.' They probably knew it was Connie, and then they said they would pay her well to strip in front of the guests at the birthday party they held for one of their friends. They were in their twenties and had just entered the tavern. But then she had to take a break with the bet again. It was reluctantly accepted, mostly because most of the men at our table also wanted to see her strip.

And after a few runs, she got herself up standing. Admittedly, she stood dangling for a bit until she found her balance. But then there were demands from that birthday party for her to get up and stand on the table so everyone could see it when she stripped. Someone helped her get onto the table.

And then she started stripping, having just knocked over a couple of beer glasses for a start. After all, she was not exactly in top form at the time. But she went to work with some slow and slightly clumsy movements. It didn't look very elegant exactly. But that wasn't so much what it came down to. It was with such rather exaggerated movements that were also about keeping the balance. It took a while, but it only made the entertainment better. People yelled and cheered every time she tore off one more piece of clothing. It was summer, and even though it was close to midnight by now, she didn't have many clothes on. But she made quite a show out of it anyway.

Finally, she stood there on the table stark naked, staggering back and forth a little, showing off all her tattoos on her arms and breasts and thighs and buttocks and other places. The cheering would never end. She had to show them all. All her roses and butterflies and red hearts and everything else, and the names of those drunken sailors, tattooed on her arms, her bosom and what not on a particularly wet night, many years ago.

But now, there were many who also wanted to hear her tell the whole story of how it had happened. The whole long, unabridged narrative. After all, she had already performed it several times in the past when she was drunk and got paid for it. She hesitated a little; I guess she didn't really bother. But when enough money came on the table, she said yes anyway. And then she told us the whole story one more time.

Of course, this also took some time. Those from the birthday party were elated. And afterward, she needed a little help getting down from the table where she had been telling her story, perhaps a little exaggerated and with some extra effects. But when she was helped down, they demanded that she walk around to each table, still naked, of course, and show her tattoos to the guests at one table after another. Back then, not many women were tattooed, so it was a bit of a sensation. That was a long before it became fashionable. At that time, nice citizens almost thought that only sailors and hookers were tattooed, although that was not entirely true.

But that whole tour provoked new cheers, and it also threw off some tips. She knew it would, so she made sure to make a little extra of it. Of course, there were also the usual suggestions that she should have some more tattoos made right away and even some offers to pay her money for it.

Some of the men asked what it would cost them if she had to have their names tattooed to complement those of the sailors and the others. But it wasn't often that she agreed to do it anymore because she had discovered that the men almost thought they owned her just because she had their name on her arm or bosom or somewhere else. I could become quite troublesome for her, so she had mostly stopped doing that again, even if she could get money for it. Now, it was only the very best and most regular customers that she gave the special favor. And only if they paid her real well for it. After all, she wasn't stupid. And she has always had a lot of business sense, no doubt about it.

But now, many of the men in the tavern demanded that she should get back to her bet again, eating that 100-dollar bill. She started putting her clothes back on. But people wouldn't put up with that. The whole tavern protested. They thought it was much more fun if she sat there and was completely naked. Or, in fact, not completely naked. She had to wear long black lacquer boots, but otherwise, she had to be completely naked. All the pub guests agreed on that. All the men, at least. But it was also the vast majority. The tavern was gradually becoming completely packed with drunken men.

But then Connie said that she would only agree to be naked, except for the lacquer boots, if each table put 250 bucks up for her. As I said, she had real business sense. Then the dollar bills got going again because the money was a bit loose after people had had a lot to drink here late in the evening. Connie went around and cashed in at all the tables.

But the men who had paid her to strip up on the table, they had become even more excited by all the things that followed, and they both wanted to have sex with her right now. They wouldn't leave her alone. They would also pay her well, they said. And Connie couldn't resist that. She walked into the back room with the two of them. Then we sat there and waited and chatted while she fixed them. Even to their complete satisfaction, from what we could understand. After all, she was a professional.

Then she came back in and sat down at the table. She was still naked, except for the boots, and had apparently come to terms with it. All the men applauded and cheered at her. And then it was time for the bet again. She tore another piece off the dollar bill and put it in her mouth. She chewed and swallowed it. It looked like she had gotten into a very good routine with it, although there was still quite a lot left. The atmosphere had gradually become quite high because a lot of people, mostly men, had come into the pub, and they had been drinking heavily for quite some time now while things about that bet kept dragging on. The tavern keeper must have had a prosperous night with something close to a record turnover.

Then she sat down and went back to work, that is, with that money bill, where there was still about half of it left to be eaten. And she really tried to approach the task a little more seriously. Slowly but surely, she ate her way through the remaining half part of the dollar bill, one small bite at a time, and helped by a lager to wash down the bits. After all, it was allowed, according to the rules they had set earlier in the evening. And she was very careful to only drink small sips so that that lager could last all the way through; she didn't want to be disqualified because she had bellowed too much beer along the way.

People watched attentively as only a little bit of that infamous dollar bill still had to be eaten. They were ready to applaud when she rather ostentatiously took the last little piece left of the note and held it up to show it off before stuffing it in her mouth. She chewed and chewed, took a few small sips of beer, and then swallowed it all. Then, the cheers broke out, and people around the table immediately declared her the winner of the bet.

But now, a new quarrel arose between the two parties to the bet. After all, they had forgotten to agree on what they were betting. At least, they claimed so now. They had been drunk even then, and of course, it had only gotten worse during the evening.

Well, they argued a bit back and forth about it. But then they agreed that the prize should be that René got a free ride with Connie. After all, it was Connie who should have received a prize because she was the one who had won the bet. But, strangely enough, they didn't think about that. Or they were just too drunk.

But Connie and René went into the back room. She was still naked, except for her boots, so they could start immediately as soon as Brian had just unzipped. The rest of us just sat drinking and chatting. There was plenty to talk about with all the evening's events, and the atmosphere was still very upbeat.

So that's how it happened that night. Afterward, the whole story has often been retold. By others and by herself when she has had something to drink. But she needed a great deal of booze before she started talking about it. She loves to brag that she knows more about money than most people do. She knows from her own experience that money doesn't smell, no matter how it's earned, even if it's by the world's oldest profession, at least she claims so, but on the other hand, it tastes like hell.

I Don't Want the Dragon, Man

Here is a note I found. It must be from around that time.

That guy, Jimmy, is very pushy. He's a pain in the ass. Men often are when they have given you a present of some kind. Then, they want something in return. They almost think they are entitled to it. And if it's a tattoo you've allowed yourself to be forced upon, then it's even worse. Then they almost think they own you.

Jimmy, he was the one who gave me that big tattoo of a dragon. By the way, it was not finished because so much else happened. He was the one who absolutely wanted to give it to me. OK, it was one I had wanted for a while because I thought it was so impressive when I saw the design drawing in the window of one of the tattoo artists. That's why I was happy when he wanted to give it to me as a present. But he doesn't own me for that reason.

Now recently, I met him again. Kind of purely by chance, one night at a tavern. I was completely done with him a long time ago. That was several years ago. It was right up to Christmas that year with all that stuff with Connie and Jansen. That's when I first met Jimmy. It never really came to anything other than a little more than a half-finished tattoo of a dragon on my stomach. He wasn't really my type. I was only interested in him at the time because he wanted to give me that big tattoo that cost a lot to get made.

But the other day, I met him again. In fact, I hadn't even

noticed that he was there until he suddenly saw me and came over to me, and pretended we were old friends, and shouldn't we just pick up where we left off then, and so on? Then he also wanted to pay to have it finished (I had a small top on with a bare stomach, so there was a clear view of most of it, except the lower part) because it was a pity that it was only half-finished. In return, I just had to do this and that and that and the third. He was full of ideas. But I didn't want any of that and said a loud and clear no to him.

Springtime Blues

This is also an old piece of text I found. I wrote it during that weird time when there so many things were breaking down.

"But summer is just about to come," Connie said.

It had been an unusually cold and grey and rainy spring, the worst in years, so all that sunny weather and hot summer days already had a lot of catching up to do. Everyone could agree to that.

It had been a while since I had last seen her, so there was a lot to talk about. But she seemed rather angry, and I think that was due to several different things I eventually found out. It wasn't just the bad weather. She was also angry that she couldn't put on her new fancy springtime dress in this cold weather. She complained about this for quite some time. After all, it wasn't that bad after all. But she kept talking about that dress, which was obviously something particularly amazing. She had found it in a small shop in a remote side street that I didn't know. One of the small, dilapidated, and run-down streets. It was a dress, which she had just found by chance one day when she came across that little shop that she didn't already know. But that dress, it was obviously just so smart and nice and whatnot, and a little daring, she said, so she just couldn't help but long to put it on and wear it.

That's how she feels sometimes. Then she gets very excited about something like that. It was going to be her springtime dress this year, she said, her symbol of springtime because it was short and tight with a deep, deep, very deep neckline in front, she said. But it was so minimal, so it was far too cold to wear in this weather. It was out of doors in the street that she wanted to flash it. If she just put on a thick sweater or coat on the outside, it wouldn't matter. And that was true.

She kept talking about that dress and the cold springtime weather and all that kind of stuff. But that dress was just the exact opposite of all her hated winter clothes, and that's why she had an almost irrepressible desire to put it on, no matter how cold and bad and all sorts of other weather it was.

Just as a symbol of springtime. To show how springtime-ready she was. How ready to throw yourself into it after the long dark winter and just give in to the long-awaited summertime? Unlike all those who keep wrapping themselves in thick winter jackets and long coats and woolen scarves well into May. Now, it should just be springtime, warm, sunny springtime, and then summer, summer, and even more summertime.

That's how she felt every spring. But it used not to be that bad anyway. Maybe she had already had a drink before I met her at lunchtime? Or was something else wrong? She was over the moon about that. Well, yes, this year, springtime had been so thoroughly delayed; I knew that. But it annoyed her beyond measure, I could understand. She can get a little moody with something like that. At least now she was angry, and she banged the table again, making it rattle and the bottles and glasses clink as if they were paid for it. And then she poured herself another whiskey. We had started out on draft beer, but she soon went up to the bar and bought a whole bottle of whiskey. It didn't look quite good, I thought. What exactly was wrong?

Now, as I said, she poured herself another whiskey. She, who otherwise never used to drink more than five–six whiskeys on the rocks before afternoon coffee. Or whatever the equivalent of it. Now, she was going off on a tangent; I was seriously afraid of that. Admittedly, she had a fiery temper, I knew that, but this seemed completely out of proportion. I couldn't get her the sunny springtime and summer weather she demanded and which everyone was longing for. Her spring longings didn't tend to be that strong. So there had to be something else at stake other than that. Although, for a long time, she kept pretending that it was just what she was upset about. I tried to ask her about it again, but she swept me off each time and continued her long rhyme about the same thing one more time. There had to be something else wrong, something more serious. But what?

I only started to get a sense of this when, after a few more whiskeys, she spilled down on herself, so her blouse got completely wet in the front, so she had to take off her blouse and wipe her breasts clean of liquor and semi-melted ice cubes. Because on each of them, there was a beautifully tattooed rose that hadn't been there a month before. Completely newly made, that is. You could see that, too. They had only just healed up recently. They were really nicely made. She always makes sure of that with what she gets done. But those newly made roses, they just sat so that they were placed at a height so that they would come fully into view in the neckline of her new naughty spring dress with the deep ringing. They were the ones she wanted to flash! Then, I could understand it a little better. But at the same time, I was also very sad and disappointed.

Well, because the two names that had been so carefully pricked into the skin of her bulging breast weren't mine. Not one of them. One of them was her own name, of course, with some curved letters with a few extra doodles on them. The name was right above the red rose, so it would be very visible in the neckline of her new dress. That was okay. But the other name was a very disgusting name, one of those names I've always tried to avoid because it reminds me way too much of a very annoying uncle I once had until he suddenly disappeared. And not enough with that. It was even worse that it also reminded me of another man. It was a guy I knew a few years ago, and he was such a jerk. And that's why I've never liked that name, and I don't think many people do these days at all. Because it's such a bad name that, hopefully, no parents will give their boys any more if they want the best for their boys and want to avoid them being teased a lot in kindergarten and school and anywhere else; imagine being called Willy.

Imagine having the name Willy tattooed on one of your breasts permanently. How can she do that to herself?

Here I go, thinking she's getting back on her feet, kind of at least, and I've helped her with that, quite a bit even, because I like her, of course, and have supported her and helped her with this and that. And then she goes and disfigures her beautiful body by having such a totally hideous loser's name etched into one of her breasts forever. Why does she do something like that? Has she crawled all the way back down to the bottom of the whiskey can, or what? I've noticed that she's started to go much harder on this lately, but I didn't think it was that bad. Can't she see how she's ruining herself?

I have fondled her beautiful breasts so often. Hundreds of times. Thousands, rather. I love them. And not just them, of course. As much as every inch of the rest of her body and her soul and everything else there is of her. Disregarding the fact that she's such a crazy weirdo sometimes. All that nonsense with those men. That is, the ones she doesn't just do it with for money, but where something like that falling in love with them comes in. It was bad enough back then with Jansen, and later, it has only gotten worse. But Jansen was before I even fell in love with her. Yes, she's a hooker, just like me, but that's okay. If only she would just keep it at that level. Then it would be more okay. Although it would probably also be good for her to stop doing so. I've told her several times to stop this man-money circus before it destroys her. She should get herself a regular job.

But she's the way that she is. What is this old saying? One time a hooker, always a hooker. I don't know if that's true. I don't like someone being judged that way in advance. But at least I know she can be as much a full-time, thoroughbred, a hundred percent hooker, but she's not a 'DIRTY RAG' like some people like to call her when they are busy slandering her. Not for me, she isn't. And not for anyone else, if I have anything to say. She's not a dirty, low-down trash-whore. She is a human being, she is a person, and she is my beloved one.

Why the hell is she doing things like that? She's done a lot of stupid, silly stuff over the years, but she's never been a dirty trash-whore. Not until now. How can she do that? After everything we've had, everything we still have together. Or maybe we don't have that anymore? What the hell is going on with her? Is it her new pimp or whatever he is, that guy Willy? Or is it a guy she's burned hot on? Connie, for Chrissake! I thought you were done with that kind of thing. Don't you remember what we talked about last spring? A year ago, almost on date. The deal we made. Doesn't it matter to you at all? Don't I matter to you anymore?

It's almost the same every spring. But this still breaks all records. And I thought you had stopped doing that after the deal we made a year ago. I really thought so. You promised me.

So that's what you needed the money for that you borrowed from me a month or so ago. The money that I had painstakingly earned by spreading my legs, but which I was just a little better at not just soldering up right away. You could borrow some money from me. To something very important, you said. So that's what you needed them for! To be disfigured with ugly and unflattering tattoos with a ridiculous name and two big red roses placed right in the neckline of that dress so anyone can see that you and Willy belong together as a couple. Because it's a boyfriend tattoo, isn't it? This is how it will be perceived by all who see it. And then even the kind you want to flash in your overly tiny, low-cut mini-dress to show everybody that now you're dating the city's biggest and most ridiculous fool. What the hell is going on with you?

It hasn't been that bad the other years. Yes, I know you have that little springtime frenzy every year. But I thought we had an agreement that you would stop being that kind of weird. Or keep it at a more reasonable level, at least. And then you just go and make it even worse and rougher and more far-fetched than ever before.

I gather that he's a real boyfriend, this Willy guy. The one you have chosen to be with instead of me. Do you really mean that? Say that it's just something you've got made when you were drunk. Say, he's just a random hooker customer! Say, it's just something you've got made for money because he paid you to get it made. Say It! But I know that's not the case. Not the way it's made.

Why can't you control that springtime frenzy? Last year, it was Brian, but that was just a name, without roses or doodles, and just kind of discreet on one upper arm. And that was only HIS name. Nothing with your own name as a counterpart. And you professed loud and holy that it was just a customer who had paid you to have his name tattooed on you. And I believed it when you said so. But maybe it was also just a lie? Pull yourself together! Please try to control your springtime feelings!

This new one with those Willy roses right in the middle of prime time in the neckline of that new dress; I won't forgive you for that. I won't! I won't!

OK, there are all the old tattoos, the ones from the time when we started down here and the time a little later when it all went off the tracks. That is one thing. I have a few of them myself. But this is something completely different. This guy, Willy. Now he thinks he owns you. But maybe he does? Maybe you are even going to marry him?

This is simply too much. What do you see in that jerk? He just wants to take advantage of you! You're aware of that, right? What the hell has he done to you? Yes, I have seen him around the pubs and how he conducts himself. He's one of those people to stay away from. Everyone I know says that. Think twice for Chrissake.

But I'm not letting you go for that reason. I just can't. I will fight for you, Connie. I'll be here when he's taken your ass off, and you're going to need me. If you still want me. I'm not letting you go. I don't just leave you to someone like him. Although that was my first reaction. I simply cannot.

Whether or not, I have to cut off my left arm. The one where I just got this done a few days ago. What I've been looking forward to showing you. Look here when I roll up my sleeve. See what it says amidst a red heart with flowers and butterflies around it. Look at what it says: Yvonne and Connie—True Love Forever. I have also been to the tattoo artist. I thought you'd be happy to see it. Does it not matter to you at all? Connie, for Chrissake.

Connie's Getting Married

And then she married him anyway, just like I had feared. That Willy guy, whom she had become so hooked on. Although I never understood what was supposed to be so amazing about that man. Or what she even saw in him.

But she wanted to get away from this place, out of the environment, and I understand that. Not least because several of the people we knew had gone all the way to the bottom.

She herself had also been well on her way. For example, there was a time when she was drunk and ate an old, greasy dollar bill because it was a bet. The whole way it was done, it was such an embarrassing performance. And she has done other things that were even worse. There were some really bad episodes. She had also started drinking a lot more. Almost every night, she was drunk.

It was far from the good old Connie. It had really gone downhill for her. It was a pity. She didn't deserve that.

Moreover, the whole environment was beginning to change. Most of it moved to another part of town, and there it was much harder. And the drugs had really come into play.

Regarding that, I understood her well. It made sense for her to want to get out of it. She had realized that it wasn't going to work here any longer. And now she acted on it. That was probably the only right thing to do. And it was that man who was supposed to help her out of it by marrying her and taking her away from the environment. But did she really need a man to help her out?

Couldn't she have done it on her own or with my help? I was more than willing to do anything to help her.

Why make herself dependent on a total loser like him? I wish she could at least have found something better. I'm afraid that she will regret it later. I'm afraid that he is going to ruin her. From bad to worse.

The idea was that they would move all the way down south. Where he came from. That means that I probably will not be seeing much of her. I am sorry about that. I'm really very sorry. But when that's what she wanted, I wouldn't stand in the way of it. I keep my fingers crossed that it will be a good thing for her and make her happy.

Then came the wedding day itself. White bride, but not a church wedding. Just at the city hall. Her parents were not there. Nor his, for that matter. Mostly some of his friends and some of those Connie knows. Of course, I was there, both at the town hall and at the wedding dinner afterward. A couple of the other girls—our colleagues—showed up at the town hall and really showed off. One in a very thigh-short red latex dress, and the other in an even more thigh-short case of some leopard-patterned metallic fabric, and both with mesh stockings and high black lacquer boots and a feather boa around the neck. It was quite festive. How people stared at the two of them, along with the rather nice and innocent-looking bride and the groom.

Afterward, there was a wedding dinner at a rather expensive restaurant. There, he behaved himself. Connie looked so happy that I almost forgave her.

The very next day, they drove down to his place down south. I think it was a house he had inherited recently. When Connie and I parted, we gave each other the longest hug in the world. We didn't want to let go of each other again. When we finally had to do it anyway, Willy looked very jealous. I bet she's never hugged him that long.

Then they drove off. I just stood there and didn't know what to make of myself. I was happy for her, of course, but sad for myself. Then I went to a bar and got drunk.

When I got the wedding picture, where she was standing beside him in her wedding dress, and she was smiling and looking so happy, I just tore the part with Willy off. I have put the part of the picture that shows Connie looking so happy in a small frame that I have on the nightstand next to my bed, so it's the first thing I see when I wake up in the morning.

Of course, we have been apart before, when I have been on re-soc or when Connie was deported to her aunt. But this is something else. More permanently. At least it is set up to be. Imagine them becoming a nice, bourgeois couple who stay together forever and celebrate their silver wedding anniversary in twenty-five years. I just can't imagine that.

But maybe that's what she needs. I can't bring myself to wish that her marriage quickly cracks and breaks down so that she comes back here. It's not a good place to be for anyone, as it's all evolving, not least after the drugs have started pouring over us. And all the betrayal that comes with it. I should also want to get away myself. But where to?

I just can't see myself in an ordinary job, having to live with some random guy that I don't feel anything for. I think this kind of life has gone into my blood.

I do hope I can come to visit her. Maybe a weekend or a week's holiday. If Willy will let me come. He seems like a rather possessive type. I don't think that he is any more positive about me than I am about him.

It can never be the same now that she belongs to someone else. Oh my god, how I miss her every day.

In the beginning, we wrote some letters to each other. She wouldn't give me their phone number so I could call her. I am sure that it is Willy that has told her. Gradually, the letters from her were sent with longer and longer intervals. After about a year, no more letters from her. And my letters started coming back, returned by the post office. Since then, I have heard nothing from her.

I don't want to talk about my own wedding and marriage. It was about a year and a half later, and it only lasted for four years. It was some guy I had met some years before, one of the people I got into trouble with at the time. The one who absolutely wanted to give me that big tattoo with that dragon design. Jimmy. And he wanted a whole lot more of me. But I didn't want to do it at that time. Then I met him again about one year ago and a few months after Connie got married. He just suddenly reappeared out of the blue. He still wanted the same thing, pretty much, plus something more. It was after Connie had disappeared from my life, and I was feeling so sad and sorry for myself. I was in a bad mood. I wasn't so critical about what I said yes to or what I did to myself. Either I had become a little more reckless, or I just didn't care about it all. So why not? Even though he was a totally far-fetched jerk. But I said yes to him and went into it with full music. It lasted just under four years. I don't want to tell you any more about it. I am not ready to do that yet.

It Wasn't You, Connie, Was It?

This is from an old piece of paper from some time back in 1980 where I've scribbled something down. But it tells something about what it was like. Something important. It's about five years after her marriage.

I keep hearing so many strange stories about Connie these days. I hope they are not right. I hope it's just loose rumors. Or that they're not about Connie at all, even though some say they are. Maybe they're just about someone else. Maybe many different girls. They are often quite vague, so it might be about her, but it might just as well be about someone else. Or maybe it's just some of those urban legends with no reality behind them. I hope so.

I'm so sorry I've completely lost touch with her. I don't even know where she is. Now, it is almost five years since she married Willy, and they moved to his place. But I don't think they live there any more. I don't know where they moved to. But from what I've heard around from time to time, he's not good to her. He takes advantage of her. He has driven her into the dirt. That is what I am hearing. That's what a lot of those stories are about. I know there's a lot of gossip. But a lot of it is about someone who might well be her and a man who could be typical of him. Many of the details fit, especially those about him, but it's still not entirely clear-cut. Or rather, not at all. It doesn't have to be them at all. I hope it is not. But there are just some of the things that almost fit a little too well. It's very confusing.

These are often stories that bear quite a lot of marks of the fact that they have been told through quite a few links and perhaps decorated along the way. I really hope that they are very much exaggerated if any of them are about Connie.

For example, I've heard quite a few stories about a couple touring the summer country up on the north coast. Some of them sound pretty much like it could be them. One is worse and more disgusting than the other. But without naming them. The description of the woman could well be Connie, and this man she is with runs a sarcastic show at her expense. She is being humiliated night after night.

The rumors are about them driving around and performing a number of degrading jokes on a flatbed truck up by the coast at the holiday resorts and all those fancy places. The man grossly humiliates the woman like a total bum, and in a way that he hands her over to the laughter of the audience in the most disgusting way. It should be extremely horrible, from what I've heard about it.

But Connie, that's not you?

Connie, where are you? Why don't I hear anything from you? Why can't I reach you? What has he done to you? Don't put up with it. Connie, tell me that you're okay and fine.

And here I am with a bottle of wine and shouting it into the night like another lunatic. But it doesn't matter if you're okay and feeling good and thriving wherever you are.

Oh, Connie…I miss you so much.

Back Then, with Candy Mommy

Sometimes, I think back to how it all started. All this stuff I've ended up in. I guess I've made some rather bad choices at times.

For example, all that stuff with Candy Mommy back then. It was totally insane. But I was young and naïve at the time. We all were. All of us who were there. All of us who let ourselves be lured into her menagerie. It was way back when I was young, long before I met Connie. But where it started to go off the rails for me.

She seemed so liberated and so progressive. Candy Mommy, as we called her. It was back in the 1960s. She rebelled against the old morality. That was one of the things that enticed us. It also appealed to the need for some excitement, of course. We were bored. We were easy to entice. But it was in a twisted way she did it. She presented it as sexual liberation.

But it was in a twisted way, where she really just took advantage of us and ushered us into something that strongly resembled a form of prostitution. That's what she did. And that was probably basically her real intention.

Under the guise of sexual liberation, she taught us to be hookers. That's what she did. She taught us a hooker's mindset and behavior and self-image. She got us used to overstepping our boundaries, step by step, until we couldn't figure out where they were going. Or if there were any direction at all. That was clearly the aim of it.

I still have her mark on my left inner thigh. Forever. And her 'sign of proficiency'. She called them that. Those stars you got tattooed on your right inner thigh when you had proven that you had overstepped one more of your limits and were prepared to go another step beyond common morality and decency. And self-respect, one might add. Once you had received five stars, you would have become a full-fledged hooker, with no – or very few – limits on what you wanted to be a part of.

Although, of course, she never said it so bluntly. I have all five of her stars on me myself. That's how it was. The reality behind all the fancy talk about sexual liberation.

The Man with the Finches

Once you got this far, you were discreetly associated with the Finch Man, as we called him. He took us a few steps further. In the wrong direction. He called us his finches. After six months in the stable with him, he claimed that we were in great demand as models and hostesses and everything. But it was a lie. At least it was only as models or at that level. Or so-called 'hostesses' in a key club. Or a so-called Champagne Girl. That's a bar girl. Or another name for a hooker. That sort of thing.

He also had a symbol that you got tattooed when you had completed the six months of apprenticeship with him. That stupid parrot you got poked into the skin on your right shoulder. Apparently, they were quite fond of that kind of thing. Then, one was 'approved' and 'recognized' (read: labeled) as one of his 'finches.'

I still have one of his silly colored parrots on my arm. He drew them up and tattooed them himself. It looks totally cracked. He had taught himself to tattoo, but he was miserable at it. He couldn't draw either, not in the normal sense.

And then he would even set himself up as an artist. And he did it too. It's almost the weirdest thing that he actually succeeded in doing it. Well, he never became a real great artist. There was always something like a charlatan about him. But for some years, he was one of the big names on the art scene. One of those that was talked about. Avant-garde artist. That's what he settled on. His ego was much bigger than his talent. But apparently, it was enough to become a fad that was on everyone's lips for a few years. The media loved him.

But he was just exploiting women – also in his art. But that wasn't so chastised back in the sixties.

He lured women to him with all the publicity he got. Young ones as well as mature women. And then, he decorated them with his 'artistic' semi-abstract drawings, which he tattooed on them. Real big drawings, sometimes over most of the body. It didn't even look like real tattoos. For a few seasons, it was the hottest thing in certain circles to have been decorated with his weird semi-pornographic crime junk all over the place. It was perceived as a work of art they had allowed themselves to be decorated with. As a symbol of how sexually liberated they were, or something like that. It caused a sensation for a couple of years, thanks to the way he staged it.

I've met a few of the women a few years later, when he wasn't in fashion any more, and they certainly regretted it a lot.

For some reason, it was only women that he wanted to decorate. It is said that they paid him with sex. He demanded that. For the month or two that he worked on them, they were to be his lover (or private hooker might be a more appropriate term) and be available to all his rather advanced desires. And as if that wasn't enough, he often had three or four women that he was working on at the same time. He was a skilled plotter, and he enjoyed pitting them against each other and making them compete fiercely to be his favorite. As a result, they became eagerly jealous of each other and would do anything they could do to slander and outmaneuver each other. Then they were better off in bed, he said. It must have been tough for them and even more so for those of them who fell in love with him. A few did. He was a pig. I personally know a few who have suffered some massive scars on their souls from the treatment he subjected them to. He was extremely gross. It was certainly not for the fainthearted.

She's a Five Star Hooker

When I am sitting here on a night like this, when the storm is raging outside, and I can't sleep, and instead I've had a glass of wine and listened to some of my favorite music, I often remember and think at times back then. A little while ago, I got to look at the weirdly crooked lines and twisted letters scratched into my left forearm. I made them myself. On a night a long time ago. That night with Suzy, who I knew all the way back from the old days. Back when I was very young, I let myself be lured into all that stuff with Candy Mommy. She had started to come to her place a little before me, and she was one of the first girls there that I got to know, and we quickly became real good friends. She was with us all the way through the maze at Candy Mommy, just like me. We had followed each other all the way through the different steps and got to know each other quite well.

Later, she had gotten well and truly into the clutches of the Finch Man, much more than me. In that respect, I was probably lucky. But she had been through the whole trip with him, too, and it hadn't been good for her. I only got there a couple of times, but she was a regular accessory.

One night, when I was there, she felt really bad. I followed her home. She was desperate and distraught. I was afraid that she would do an accident to herself. In any case, she was very distraught. I tried to get her drunk with whiskey to get her to fall asleep, but she could tolerate a lot, and I had to keep up with it myself.

At one point, she took a sharp knife and began to cut herself, apprehensively near the wrist. I knew there would be no point in trying to persuade her not to. It would just make her defiant. I had to come up with something else. It was those crooked lines I still have tattooed on my left forearm.

And she has some similar ones.

I told her to see what you could do with that knife. I had her give me the knife, and I scratched a few crooked lines into my arm. It should say the word 'LOVE,' but it is difficult to read. Then I took some black color from her desk and rubbed it in. I said we should take turns tattooing on each other as a symbol of our friendship. As a start, she had to give it a try on my arm. I told her how to alternate one letter at a time. It was simply to make her do something else with that knife and to emphasize that I was there for her.

It worked for a while. But then she started wanting to do something for herself, and then it became dangerous again. The next time I got hold of the knife, I yelled, "Have you seen what I can do? Do you think I can hit that tree out in the yard?" She lived on the first floor, and out in the yard, there was a big old tree. I opened the window and hurled the knife at the tree with all my might. And bingo, it drilled into the trunk and stayed stuck three–four meters up in the tree trunk. Of course, I had first made sure that there was no one down in the yard who could get hit by it.

In that way, we got rid of the knife. But now I had to come up with something more, just as I kept pouring whiskey on her to make her fall over drunk. But it was harder than I had expected, and I also had to keep up to make it look natural.

But I knew she played a little guitar like myself and many others back then. I pulled her guitar off the wall, started strumming on it a little bit, and began singing a self-composed little song that I made up on the spot to cheer her up a bit.

It went something like this.

She is having a hard time. She is in trouble.

But she is a Five Star Hooker, and she knows what to do.

She has been fighting hard, but she can take it.

Cause she is a Five Star Hooker, and she knows what to do.

She is out on a hard road, but she is out to win.

For she is a Five Star Hooker, and she knows what to do.

And some more verses in the same style.

The words Five Star Hooker referred to the fact that we both had all five stars tattooed on the inner thigh from the old days as a symbol that we had been through all the steps of Candy Mommy's hard school and had been approved as full-fledged hookers.

I think it cheered her up a bit. I came up with about nine verses. Probably they were not verses, and maybe it wasn't exactly brilliant, and I don't remember them all.

Fortunately, the whiskey was now also starting to work on her. Eventually, she went out like a candle, and I helped her into bed and tucked her under the covers so she wouldn't wake up in the middle of the night and feel cold.

Then I removed all the sharp knives in the kitchen and took them with me in my bag. Next stop was the medicine cabinet. There were some painkillers and stuff like that. I emptied them all except for one glass. I had just bought some zinc pills for colds and had them in my bag. They were the same color and shape, so I swapped them up and put the medicine glass down on the bathroom floor, so it looked like I had dropped it when I cleared the medicine cabinet. If I removed it all, she might go over to the pharmacy and buy some new ones if she had those kinds of thoughts. Now, I bet she would take my harmless zinc supplement pills instead.

Then I just checked that she was sleeping soundly and well, and then off to my home. It was getting late. For the next few days, I stopped by as often as I could, and it seemed that she had gotten over the worst and was getting better. We stayed in touch for a while. Then she went to college, a long course of six–seven months, and I think that was good for her.

An Interview about My Art Projects

And now, I will jump forward in time to where I am now. That is, in the latter half of the 1990s. I have succeeded with my art projects; there is no denying it. I am completely out of the old environment and am today a recognized artist in my special field. I can say that. Although many also perceive my art projects as provocative. But to me, they make perfect sense, and they pull full houses every time. The following is a transcript of a telephone conversation between Marianne and me, written out for this context. It's only after I've been doing those performance events for a few years. Of course, it started out much more modestly and only gradually evolved into what it has become today here in the late 1990s. At first, it was difficult to find a place that would add premises. A lot of people thought it was too provocative.

M: "Hi, it's Marianne."

Yvonne: "Hey! Long time no see. How's Kevin doing?"

M: "Oh, forget it. He is in the past. I have already moved on. But how did your art exhibition go?"

Y: "It went rather well. He was a bit difficult at first, but later, we got a really good working relationship around it."

M: "Was he decorated all over?"

Y: "No, I don't use full-body designs that much anymore." It's all too easy to just look like porridge after a few years. If it's too massive. The Japanese can make it almost as a kind of bodysuit, which is very carefully composed and with some large lines in the design. They are the champions in that field. I did it a few times in the beginning, but now I'm experimenting a little more with the expression I want to bring out.

M: "You split it up a bit more, I mean graphically?"

Y: "You could say that. I think it's much nicer if there's some bare skin in between. Then, the individual parts of the design look more impressive, I think."

M: "What about that new, very geometric style? What do you think of that? Does it inspire you?"

Y: "No, not real. Some of it looks great, but it's not exactly my style. I'm pretty much inspired by old school. The old-school sailor tattoos had something special about them, I think. That's often where I get my inspiration from."

M: "What was the theme this time?"

Y: "The latest one here has a big octopus that wraps its tentacles around most of its body. And then with a little waves and foam splashes all around. Each of the octopus's tentacles then holds a naked or half-naked female. I think that tells a lot about him. I had told him beforehand that he was going to send me some of the movies that he's been drooling over the most. And if he had a special favorite scene in them. Then I drew some of the women from there up in such a kind of cartoon style as some really exaggerated pinups. I made quite a few of those drawings. There were probably about thirty of them to choose from. The intention was that the audience at the art exhibition where he was exhibited could decide which ones of the drawings he should have tattooed. After all, only ten were needed. It was usually the most extreme of them that the audience preferred. One of them each night of the exhibition. Then, it was tattooed right away, and the audience could follow it on a big screen. Afterward, the title of the movie from which the female character in question came was tattooed next to it in some small, nice decorative letters."

M: "How does it work when the audience gets to choose which drawing it should be?"

Y: "This time, the show lasted two weeks, and ten of the days, he got one of those women tattooed on him. The big octopus itself that wraps around his entire body, that one I had almost finished beforehand. He had first had a whole series of sessions at my house, also so that I could get to know him properly – and he could get to know me – so I could make the perfect design for him. And explained to him how it was all supposed to happen so he knew it in advance. He agreed, of course, with everything."

M: "But how did it happen on each of the evenings when the audience had to choose? After all, it was something that would affect him forever!"

Y: "Of course, that's what attracted the audience. What fascinated them and really got some of them up and running. There was a strong element of some hardcore reality coming in here."

And that's one of the things the audience is most excited about today, I can promise you that. That's probably why it's become such a big success. That kind of thing can really get people out of their chairs. They don't really want such an old-fashioned art exhibition any more. Where you just walk around and look at some pictures or installations. It's just too boring. Something more is needed in subjects if it is to capture enough interest. Something more dramatic. Something irrevocable. It's a real hit.

M: "But how exactly did it happen? Did the audience vote for it?"

Y: "No, it probably would have been too boring. There

should preferably be a little more drama about it. Some excitement about what it will be next. And it should be stretched out a little so that the decision does not come too quickly. There should be a slightly longer process where people can follow it and get excited about it. Many have their own favorite among the options that are and hope that it will be, or that it certainly won't be, that other one that they think is horrible, or too tame, or too violent, or something else entirely. It was sold at an auction, so the highest bidder decided which one of the thirty drawings should be tattooed on his body. Of course, all drawings were shown all the time on some big screens, and those who made a bid had to decide that it was this and that drawing they made a bid for. You should have seen what a great atmosphere it created in the audience! Something completely different from an old-fashioned dusty painting exhibition. Much more in tune with our times. But it is probably not exactly something you should invite your mother-in-law to see. It was amazing! When someone came up with a higher auction bid for a certain one of those pinup drawings, that is, the one, the man was supposed to have tattooed a little later in the evening, that drawing flashed up on the big screen along with the amount that had been offered. And then, of course, there were at least a few who wanted it to be one of the other drawings, and then a bid came in for one of them, and then it flashed up on the big screen along with the amount that had been offered for it. It was a fixed rule that at least 50 Dollars had to be bid above the previous bid. You can believe that the commandments got going! The audience usually were divided into five–six teams, each with its own favorite drawing and cheering eagerly every time it was offered a higher bid, and vice versa; they whistled and shouted out loud when one of the other was in focus. This was for real. I think it will be the kind of event of the future in the field of art. So that the audience really gets engaged in what's going on and is actively involved in the process. That way, they get a much greater experience out of it. It's time for the art world to keep up with the times of the modern world. After all, we don't live in Rembrandt's time any more. It was, of course, organized so that the tension was not released too quickly. As a rule, it took a full hour before the auctioneer could give a hammer blow on who the winner of the evening was. She or he who had bid the highest and thus won the auction. Then she was cheered by his supporters and pointed the finger at by those from the other teams – those who wanted it to be another drawing that won. There was a bit of commotion there. But it has only happened a few times that there have been fights between the different groups. It is mostly in the evenings when there are many men in the audience. But the museum has, of course, provided a large team of security guards who can intervene and stop this kind of thing before it degenerates. But as I said, it's not that often it happens. After that, we just try to get the audience to calm down before it goes further on. There will be a break where champagne and some delicious tapas or sushi and various other things will be served, and people can also mingle and maybe make some new acquaintances with some other art enthusiasts.

"Or maybe find a new girlfriend, or just someone to take home to bed afterward, or go out into the city with, or whatever you feel like. And after the auction, where most people have been up and running, I promise that the ice has been broken and people are mingling on their own. I've heard a lot of people say that if you have a little class and want to find a boyfriend or partner or bedmate who also has a little class, this is much better than going to a bar or a disco and whatever else there is."

M: "Does it never happen that one of the women falls in love with him or that he starts taking on one of them?"

Y: "Oh, it happens a lot. But he must not do anything in relation to women. For example, invite them out. Or do something else to start a relationship. This is not at all part of his role in the exhibition."

M: "What if there are two or three women in the audience who start competing for him? Has that ever happened?"

Y: "Yes, several times. It can be rather difficult to handle."

M: "Some people would say you're taking advantage of men."

Y: "Do you know what I and many others think in everyday life about the men who exploit women? Both as sex objects and in all sorts of other ways. I think that it is a very mild shade of what countless women have been exposed to. Don't forget that the men themselves have said yes to it.

"Don't forget that it's a work of art they get to help create. Then someone will say that the men are exhibited, both in the cage there at the exhibition itself and afterward at the films about it. Yes, but think of all the women who have put up with being models over the years. Then this is no worse.

"On the contrary, that's a much milder version of it. A pure luxury version in comparison. They just get a small hint of it. That's all."

To Connie

Connie, this book was written for you. I have written a book about our life together back then and about myself and my own life. How it has been. Maybe it's gotten a little messy, a little unsystematic. But then, that's the way it is. That's as good as I can do it. But Connie, I hope you're somewhere out there feeling good and happy with your life. I haven't been able to track you down anywhere. I've been around the environments from back then. But they have changed a lot. No one really knew anything about you. Only some old stories that you had gone to the bottom and gone all the way down into the dirt. But that's not true, is it? It's just stupid gossip, right?

I just hope that's the way it is. And Connie, I hope I haven't contributed to anything bad for you. Not with my goodwill. But that I've pushed you to a bad place. I hope not.

Connie, this book is for you. It's you I wrote it for. I hope one day you will come across it somewhere, in a bookstore, in a library, at a friend's house, or read about it online. And that you remember me and remember the things we've had together and forgive me if I've happened to do some things that weren't very good for you. I think of you often. I hope that one day I will hear from you. If you feel like it.

And now comes the most important thing in this book. I've saved it for the last page. Here it comes,

Connie, I love you.